MURDER ON SACRED GROUND

A Reverend Calvin Turkstra Mystery

Christopher H. Meehan

Thunder Bay Press

Murder on Sacred Ground

Published by
Thunder Bay Press
Holt, MI 48842

First edition
First printing, 2006

ISBN 10: 1-933273-07-4
ISBN 13: 987-1-933272-07-8

This is a work of fiction: names, characters,
places and incidents either are products of the
author's imagination or are used fictitiously. Any
resemblance to people, living or dead, is entirely
coincidental.

Printed in the United States of America

"When they had crucified him, they divided up his clothes by casting lots."

Matthew 27:25

To Jack

I would like say to thank you to a couple of folks, including Sam Speigel and Julie Taylor at Thunder Bay Press, Richard Jordan, the cover artist, Andy Angelo, the copy editor, Brad Pines, the photographer for my headshot, Scott Harmsen, the guy who told me to keep going when I wanted to stop, to Agnes Birnbaum and Janet Benry who gave me advice at crucial places, and to a Kalamazoo mystery writer's group who helped me get some important things right.

Thanks.

CHAPTER ONE

I was tired and not up to driving into Grand Rapids so late on a Sunday night. But I had made a promise to a dying father, and I take things like that pretty seriously.

So, we whipped off U.S. 131 at Wealthy Street and soon the Cathedral of Saint Barnabas, one of the largest and oldest of the downtown churches, loomed straight ahead, its spires rising imposingly against the dark October sky.

On the seat next to me sat Bob Smit, my girlfriend's brother—a crazy and lovable kid in a man's body. We'd come here to meet a man who promised information about the murder of Melinda Blackwell, the adopted daughter of a Christian Reformed Church pastor—the man to whom I'd made the promise. Melinda's bludgeoned body was found floating in Gun Lake a few weeks before.

Just as the caller had told me on the phone, he had parked his Ford Festiva near the sidewalk that led to one of the side doors of the cathedral.

Following instructions, I flashed my headlights twice, and waited. But no one emerged from either the car or the shadows surrounding the cathedral.

I wasn't sure what to make of it. Clearly, the man had been anxious to talk about the $25,000 reward I had recently offered, asking for information leading to the arrest of Melinda's killer. More than that, he said he had something important he wanted to give me.

Why the caller chose here wasn't clear. I had asked him to drive to my small church in Wayland. We could talk after I finished with the Sunday night youth-group Bible study. But he insisted that we meet in Grand Rapids.

"Let's check out the car, but you stay close," I told Bob.

Once we hit the sidewalk, Bob's nostrils flared. Wind shot around us, whipping leaves from trees lining the street. Bob pinched his nose and then waved an arm. He had been born with a strange mental malady. At times he made sense, while at others he seemed lost in his own world.

"What is it?" I asked.

He shook his head, making a pained face and pointing at the Festiva.

I sniffed a couple of times and then caught the odor of pot, coming from inside the car. I stepped up to the driver's side and looked through the rolled-down window.

I saw mounds of fast food wrappers, empty beer cans and a map on the front seat. By the strength of the marijuana odor, I figured the driver had to have been here not too long before. Maybe being high on pot explained his absence.

I shut the door, looking around, hoping to spot someone in the dim light spilling from an incandescent street lamp attached to the pole near my truck. I saw no one, except for Bob lumbering like a big kid down the sidewalk toward the church.

"Hey, where are you going?" I asked as he picked up his pace, crossing a patch of lawn and heading for steps that led to a side door of the cathedral.

"Bob!"

He stopped on the second step, calling, "Lookee!"

Unable to see what he meant, I trotted over.

"See!" he said when I joined him on the steps.

"What?"

"Stupid!" he answered, more insistent.

Then I saw it—a slop of liquid, by one of his feet. I felt my heart catch.

Before I could stop him, Bob bent, dipped a finger in the fluid, made a face and offered me a lick.

"Stop it!" I said.

On my knees, I got a better look. Years ago I had served as a paramedic. A memory flashed through my mind—of a man who had blown his brains out behind a bar. What I saw that night looked similar to the blob of material on the step. "My God," I gulped.

Squinting, I saw dark splotches leading up the final steps to the porch. From there, they crossed the cement to where Bob now stood by the door to the church.

"Bob, don't touch anything," I said.

But he didn't listen. He reached for the handle, yanked the door open and, before I could call him back, raced inside. What in the world was that door doing open? I wondered.

Following him in, I called Bob's name, but I heard no answer.

Votive candles flickered, casting long shadows on the tile walls as I pushed through a pair of doors and into the nave. I smelled incense. Then I heard a door open and spotted Bob dart into the gloomy sanctuary. "Get back here!"

Slipping by the bank of candles, I went after him and into the church proper. Red exit signs above the doors gave some light. Even so, everything was without distinct shape or character. Shadows blanketed the pews; gloom hung everywhere.

"Bob!"

Pews ran on all sides. Wide, round pillars separated the sanctuary and blocked my view of the chancel as I stepped carefully across the back. A baptismal font, about the size and shape of a large hot tub, stood directly in my path. I didn't like this.

My eyes swept the side aisles for any sign of Monica's brother. I called again, this time louder. "Bob, dang it, where are you?"

Something or someone scraped across the floor up by the altar dais.

I spun that way, catching quick, shifting movement in the asp beyond the altar, just below the hanging crucifix. I felt a stirring in the air, and caught whiff of an odor I couldn't place. "Bob!"

Then I heard shuffling, and turned to the right just in time to see a dark form lunge from a pew. I tried to dodge the attacker, but failed.

He slammed into my back. The force sent me tumbling. My legs went out and my head cracked something hard. I saw flashes of light.

I felt in a weirdly blessed state, as if I hung in suspended animation. Images floated in and out, none that made any sense.

When I came to, after what had to have been only a few moments, Bob knelt next to me. His moon-shaped face peered down, his eyes darting, his hands shaking as if they were on fire.

"Who hit me?" I asked, not really expecting an answer.

"Big oaf," he answered, haphazardly shaping a figure with his hands.

For a second, I wondered if he was the oaf. Maybe Bob had barreled into me by mistake in the dark and didn't want to admit it. Then I thought of that movement on the altar. If that had been Monica's brother, I'd been body-blocked by someone else. My head ached and my eyes kept slipping in and out of focus. I tried to recall what I saw of that form that flew at me from the pews.

Bob got up and started to wander away.

I let him go and tried to assess my injuries. Everything seemed to be intact, although my head hurt.

Getting up and starting to walk, I had a better view of the church, especially by the front altar, where Bob stood, looking down.

Then I heard a bump and thud along a side aisle. Bob swung that way, apparently saw something, and took off. I tried to run, but my head spun, and I had to hold back a second. The world looped and spun, making me feel nauseous. The floor dipped and steadied.

Bob started screaming, "I'm coming to get to you!" A moment later he slammed through a door and raced into the night.

Monica's brother was panting, hands on his hips, when a few moments later I stepped onto the stone porch fronting South Division Avenue, the main drag running north and south through Grand Rapids. We'd come in on the other end of the church.

A siren now wailed and the lights of a fire truck from the central station house flashed along the avenue.

Just as the fire engine blasted by, Bob sprang to life. With the grace of a much lighter man, he leapt off the porch and crashed through bushes, returning to the front of the cathedral. It wasn't worth ordering him to stop.

Instead, I hobbled after him, taking a stone path across the side lawn, along the edge of the church and its darkened stained glass windows. I put my hand to my head and felt a lump.

Headlights swept through the air as I reached the front.

Monica's brother stood in the street next to my Ranger and directly in the path of the Festiva.

CHAPTER TWO

About a quarter mile ahead, the Festiva started to swing through what we in Michigan's second largest city call the S-curve, a death trap sweeping in four quick turns through downtown. Recently redone by the state, it remained a crazy every-man-for-himself racecourse.

But traffic wasn't bad at 10 p.m. on a Sunday night, and so I didn't have to worry too much about sideswiping anyone or getting bashed from behind as we corkscrewed along U.S. 131.

Bob rocked back and forth, his face reflecting the tension of this ride. He had dodged the car before I could reach him outside the cathedral. We then climbed in my truck and gave chase. I wasn't sure what I wanted, except to get close enough to see who was driving or at least get the license plate number. Or, assuming this had been my assailant, maybe I could get a little payback by ramming him into the median.

My truck's underbelly rattled. The shocks needed replacing. We were now heading north, cutting along the edge of the West Side, the oldest part of town, full of aging furniture factories. The river rolled by on our right. The Festiva had slowed. It dipped in and out of sparse traffic ahead of me. Maybe he didn't know I was back here.

If I had my cell phone, I would have used it, but I had left it at church. Monica's brother waved a hand in the air, as if warding off a smell. "Ditching us," he said.

That taillight had vanished. But as we came over a small rise near Riverside Park, I caught a glance of the Festiva turning onto the ramp to I-96, the freeway that went east to Lansing. The longer the chase lasted, the more I wanted to catch that guy, and the more I realized how stupid this was.

The Festiva cut onto I-96, where the freeway re-crossed the Grand River and shot by the graveyard of the Michigan Home for Veterans. I was right after him.

That one taillight was putting more distance between us, and I gunned the gas, wondering who was in that car. Questions formed and fled as I drove closer. I wanted answers, and not just to whom had jumped me in church.

"Dummy!" Bob smacked the dashboard and pointed.

The Festiva whipped into the far right lane, just as we intersected with the Gerald R. Ford Freeway, and was now headed toward the East Beltline exit.

I had to dodge cars coming hard on the road named after our native son who took over the Oval Office when Tricky Dick went down the tubes. Horns blared as I turned the wheel toward the ramp leading off the freeway and onto the Beltline.

Bob had his face glued to the windshield as I made it with just enough room to bounce up and onto the exit.

Craning up in my seat, I saw the Ford turn south. This stretch was fairly busy, and a light rain started to fall, giving a slick sheen to the pavement.

The Ranger's back wheels felt like hard unforgiving rubber, and the truck bed bounced without much give as I chased the Festiva through the caution light at Cascade Road.

When I nearly rear-ended a car that appeared out of nowhere, I realized trying to keep up with the fleeing Festiva really was nuts. I needed to find a phone and call this in. What the cops might find if they stopped the car was hard to say. Plus, I needed to calm down.

But I also needed, if nothing else, the Festiva's license plate number.

At the next light, just before Calvin College, instead of shooting south toward the bright lights of 28th Street, the Festiva braked and hung a right, heading into a neighborhood behind the college.

I swung that way, skidded on the wet pavement, almost went sideways through the intersection and nearly front-ended a Camry.

Lights flashed through my truck, and I slammed into a curb.

Bob was pounding the windshield.

Maybe 50 yards in front of us, the Festiva turned into a back entrance to the college. I slammed down the gas pedal.

Twenty minutes later, Bob and I stood by the Festiva that had been abandoned in the parking area for the Calvin nature preserve, which ran into an undeveloped area behind the married housing apartments. I thought I was right on his tail, but the driver had already fled from the car by the time I pulled in. We ran down the path 100 yards or so into the nature preserve, hoping to find the driver, but had no luck and returned here.

Lights from a Grand Rapids police cruiser and a Calvin College security patrol car flickered in the air. Both were parked near my truck.

The college security officer, a guy named Sonny, had come on us soon after I pulled in. The city cop wasn't far behind. A few minutes before, I had asked Sonny to use his cellular phone to make a call. The same phone now rang in my hand.

"So Turkstra, who's the dead guy in the cathedral?" demanded the familiar voice on the other end.

It took a second for this to settle, but even then it made no sense. "You found a body?"

"Yes, sir. Dead as can be."

"Are you sure?" I asked stupidly.

Captain Manny Rodriguez, head of the Grand Rapids Police Department's Major Case Team, assured me I had nothing wrong with my hearing. Using 911, I had asked for him to call Sonny's cell phone. If nothing else, I wanted his advice.

"The first units on the scene tell me there's a corpse in there, right by the altar," Manny said.

"You're not there yet?"

"Just pulling up."

"Any idea who is it?" I asked.

"I'll bet it isn't Jesus."

My heart beat fast and my mind raced, trying to recall what had been in that church. I now recalled Bob at the altar looking down. When I left, I scooted through some pews halfway down the aisle, bypassing the area near the altar.

"So what's going on, Reverend?"

Bob was peering in the windows of the Festiva, his pants hanging low and showing white skin. The two cops were conferring. "I didn't see anybody," I responded, thinking about that blood on the sidewalk. I suddenly felt weak.

"Talk to me, Turkstra."

I explained to Manny what had happened, in detail from start to finish. He was talking on his cell phone, and static kept cutting in on us. But I got it out.

Manny was still peppering me with questions, like why did I leave the cathedral and so on, when another two more cruisers and a big car pulled in. The cruisers stopped a few yards away. But the car screeched to halt not too far from me. The door of the Caprice flew open and Grand Rapids Police Chief Ray Kroger emerged. He glared and headed directly for me. To say the least, we aren't friends.

"What's the police chief doing here?" I asked Manny.

"He's there?"

"In all of his glory."

"He's the boss."

When Kroger found out who was on the line, he ripped the phone from me and began barking orders at Manny.

A fine misty rain still fell. I turned and gazed into the woods. Crickets and other critters made noises in the dark. I heard cheeps and chirps, and thought I saw bats flitting in and out of the trees. Deeper in came a soft mournful moan, as if the ground itself was in pain. Reminding me of a tracking dog on a leash, Bob kept edging toward the woods, but the Calvin cop held him back.

"Turkstra!" The Chief stood a foot or two away. Behind him a Grand Rapids cop shined his flashlight in the Festiva. Other cops, having emerged from their cruisers, moved off into the woods, also

13

using flashlights. Bob went with them. Sonny gave me the OK sign, signaling he had an eye on Bob, as they started down the path. "What were you doing in the cathedral?" asked Kroger.

"Saying the rosary?"

"You're not Catholic. Cut the crap."

In some ways on some days, Chief Kroger could be refreshing, as long as you were on his side. He had a nearly bald, bullet-shape head, gravelly voice and eyes that looked crazy, cruel and calculating at the same time. Those eyes now ate me up, his chest swelling inside the starched blue uniform shirt. He and I had clashed a few times. Once, not long ago, it happened when I put in to be a police chaplain. He nixed it because he said he didn't trust me, saying I was more inclined to side with the troublemakers than the ones paid to put them in jail. I guess he probably had a point.

"Did you just happen to be in the neighborhood, Chief?" I asked.

"Tell what happened, Reverend."

I gave him a quick rundown on the same things I'd told Manny.

He listened, swore, badgered me with his own questions, and then moved off to confer with the first cop on the scene.

Unsure of my role here, I stepped over and leaned against my truck. Rubbing the knot on my head, I wondered if I'd abandoned someone who was dying or already dead. But still, I had seen no body. Then I thought again of the blood on the sidewalk and I grew sick in my stomach.

A group of cars carrying gawkers had started to line the perimeter of the parking lot by the street.

"What the hell!" I then heard.

It was Kroger, heading in my direction. I braced myself, but he ran by me, gesturing at a big, shambling figure that had just burst from the woods, a couple of cops in hot pursuit.

I saw Bob, running along with a big garbage bag hugged to his chest.

Cops quickly surrounded him, hiding him from view. A couple started to raise their flashlights. "Hey, hold it!" I yelled.

14

Kroger got there before me, shouting at Bob, demanding to know what was happening.

Bob screamed right back, although he wasn't using words. Things were getting real hot when I shoved into the middle of the fracas. I did my best to try to negotiate a peace. But it wasn't easy. Once the cops finally got the bag and looked into it, it became clear that it contained more than garbage. Exactly what it was, they refused to tell me. They had the evidence technician carefully wrap and carry it away.

After that, it was more of the same. I had to go over and over what I had seen.

CHAPTER THREE

Going on midnight, I pulled up to the cathedral and stepped out of my truck, I was struck by the difference. Not long before, the area had been dark and quiet. No longer.

Bright lights from a Grand Rapids Police Forensics Department van lit the entire north side of the cathedral. A group of evidence technicians stood on the sidewalk where I'd spotted blood. On the far side, by the back door we had exited, stood an ambulance, its lights flipping in the air. Cops and detectives were either milling about or moving in and out of the church.

The rain had stopped and a soft breeze had started. Wrapping my arms around my chest, I scanned the area for Manny. Unable to spot him, I stepped away from my Ranger, in which Bob snoozed away in the front seat.

Still unable to see Manny, I started off to ask one of the cops to track down my friend.

I hadn't gone far when Barry Lazio, the mayor of Grand Rapids, appeared from out of a small crowd lining the sidewalk leading to the side door Bob and I had gone through a couple of hours before.

"Calvin, how are you?"

"I've been better."

"The cops say you found the body in there."

"Not me."

"But you were in there when it happened?"

I knew that Barry lived nearby in a revamped mansion in the Heritage Hill Historic District. I suspected he heard the action on the police scanner and walked down the hill to check it out. But it sounded like he'd already been more than just a bystander.

He and I went way back—to the rolling farm land west of here, to the area around the tiny burg of Vriesland, a town settled 135 years ago by my Dutch ancestors who fled to the New World in the wake of poverty and religious persecution in The Netherlands.

We lost touch about the time of the Vietnam War and got reacquainted a few years ago.

"Does this have to do with that reward I saw you talking about on TV?" Barry asked, nodding at the cathedral.

"I need to talk to Manny Rodriguez. Have you seen him?"

"I haven't."

Lazio was shorter than my 6-foot-2-inch frame. And the difference only started there. He had jet black, slicked-backed hair, while mine was dust-colored and long enough to be tied in a pony tail. His skin was swarthy, his brown eyes sharp and perceptive, and his manner blunt and aggressive. I was pale-skinned, blue-eyed and tended toward shyness—unless my dander got going—like if you slammed into me in a dark church.

Barry wore a short-waisted brown leather coat, over a T-shirt, beige slacks and loafers without socks. The son of a butcher, who was Christian Reformed, and a Catholic mother, he had done very well for himself, Notre Dame Law School and all.

"Can you at least tell me what in the hell has happened here?" Barry waved a hand at the church, his square jaw upturned.

"It sounds like you've already been talking to someone, Barry."

Lazio threw me an irritated look, the same one I'd seen him give judges when he was prosecuting a case in local district court. We had faced off a few times over cases involving my parishioners when I served a storefront church not far from where we now stood. Then, after leaving the law and becoming mayor, that expression often crossed Barry's well-shaved face during city council meetings when rabble-rousers such as myself had showed up to complain. "Look, Calvin, I'm only trying to find out what happened." His eyes gave me their patented nailing-you-to-the-wall look.

"Barry, it's been a bad night. You'll need to get it all from the police," I said, starting to turn away.

He grabbed my arm. "Calvin, what happened in that church?"

I saw something more than curiosity on his face. Lazio looked worried and maybe even upset over what might have happened to the guy in the church.

"I don't really know. Someone jumped me when we went in, and then we chased him. I didn't see a body when I was in there."

He stepped closer, an edgy hint of anxiety in his eyes. "Who was killed?"

"I don't know!"

"Who jumped you?"

"No idea."

Barry moved back, sticking his hands over his chest and gazing at the church. Then he made the sign of the cross. In my case, I assumed the Calvinist faith of my pious father, while Barry went the way of Rome—hence his love for the Fighting Irish, and of course the rote religious gesture now.

"Reverend?"

I felt a tap on my back. It was Manny, who nodded at the mayor.

"Do you have any idea who the victim is, Captain?" Lazio asked the detective.

"Only that he's dead, sir."

"Who found the body?"

"The janitor."

Lazio stiffened slightly and narrowed his eyes. He seemed to swallow some shock and fear before speaking. "It's the cathedral, for Christ sake."

Manny shot me a fast look and then jerked his head, gesturing for me to stand off to the side.

The detective and the mayor talked for a couple minutes. They stood under the branches of a large tree, a streetlight catching the irritation in Manny's stance and what I took to be high-level interest in the mayor's.

We were in front of the cathedral, near where the Festiva and my

18

truck had been parked earlier. Several of the locals gathered in small groups along the sidewalk and in the stone courtyard separating the cathedral from the nearby parish grade school. Above us rose the slender spires of the cathedral, their tips pointing at a murky purplish sky.

I stepped over and checked on Bob. He was still asleep.

Then for a moment I closed my eyes, replaying my time in the church, getting body slammed. I tried to picture who had done it. Out of the corner of my eye I had caught something—a large form, maybe, flying hair, and possibly even the smell of booze. These images floated back, and I wondered if I was making them up.

"Hey, Reverend, this is no time for meditation."

Manny was back, swaying his bantam rooster body on feet which, as always, were encased in highly polished, hand-tooled cowboy boots.

"The mayor is bothered that somebody got blood all over the church," I said, noticing Lazio huddled in a group of cops and, it looked like, a priest or two, and a tall, long-haired guy I think was the church janitor.

"C'mere, there's something I want you to see."

"Let me check on Bob again." Luckily, I spotted Gerry DeHaan, a former church member, and asked him to keep an eye on my slumbering sidekick.

Five minutes later, I took a peek under the mortician's blanket covering the victim. I struggled to stand still and stared at the face resting immobile on the gurney, its skin drained of color, the harsh light from portable police generators giving the man's long, sharp-featured face a harsh, oatmeal-like quality. One side of the head was a smashed pulp, the other intact.

"You know him?" asked Manny.

"He doesn't look familiar."

I bent to take a closer look, noticing a splash of long black hair, a large nose, and a slightly pocked face.

"Your mystery caller?" asked Manny.

"Maybe."

"But you say he told you he was driving a Festiva?"

I nodded.

"Did he say he was alone?"

I shook my head.

One of the paramedics had a hold of the blanket. He let it drop after Manny gave him the nod. We stepped back and watched as they hoisted him into the ambulance. This was a familiar scene for me—carting away the maimed and the dead in the wake of some awful event.

The medics positioned the gurney, readjusted the blanket, belted the body in and closed the door. We backed away as the ambulance started to roll carefully away from the cathedral.

Manny indicated for me to follow him around the side of the church, away from the crowd and near the back entrance used in the dead of winter as a clothing bank.

We stood between tall bushes, the church and sidewalk fronting on Division. "Where was the body, Manny?"

"Let me ask the questions, Reverend."

I buttoned my lips as Manny took a few moments to try to read me the riot act, starting in on asking what was I doing here and such. Didn't I know a body lay in there? What was I thinking chasing the car? But I didn't let it go very far.

"Manny, what good does yelling at me do now?"

"Who's yelling?"

"You are!"

Well, we both were.

The cop's eyes nailed into me. "Why'd you go in there anyway?"

"Blood led to the door. It was open. Bob went in and I followed."

He spat at ground. "That's the blind leading the blind." The cop then turned and faced the church, rearranged the cap on his head.

Manny was a scrappy cop. He had gone through two marriages as he moved through the ranks in a dozen years from patrolman. He had a son who had a disease similar to Bob's, and, although he was once again single, he managed to raise the boy by himself, with help from his mother. In a softer voice, he said, "Go over it again."

As I did, he listened carefully. When I had finished, he began to pace. I noticed a couple detectives waiting on the sidewalk, obviously wanting to talk to him. But he ignored them, walking a half-circle around me before stopping. "You know what I think, Reverend?" He paused, maybe for effect, but maybe not. His voice was pitched low, but it carried anger and accusation. "How about this? What if that poor bastard was just a dope-head who really knew nothing and just wanted your reward money that you so illustriously offered all over the news."

"If he didn't know anything, why kill him?"

"Maybe because he got in the way."

"In the way of what?"

Manny was hotter than I'd seen him in awhile. "Maybe we'll never know. Because he's too dead to ask."

He backed off, but not for long. "Why didn't you just leave it alone?"

I knew what he meant—the press conferences, the column I helped steer into the newspaper, and most recently the reward.

"What am I supposed to do, Manny?"

"Jesus Jenny, let the police do their job. It's not your Christian duty to solve the murder."

"I knew Melinda. She had come to me."

Manny raised an eyebrow, took a couple of breaths. "You say your caller knew her?"

"It sounded like he did."

"You believed him?"

"I had to check it out."

Manny checked the sky, and then looked back at me. "He told you, what, that he knew who killed her?"

"He strongly suggested it."

"And he told you he had something that you might want?"

"He had."

"But he didn't say what it was?"

"That's when he said we had to meet if I wanted to learn more."

21

"You know," said Manny, "you're going to need to make a statement."

"I thought I was just doing that?'

"God, you're a pain."

CHAPTER FOUR

I stood at the window of my second-floor apartment, above the tavern downstairs, staring at Main Street. Just down the way winked the red lights atop the silos of the flour mill. Across the street stretched a row of mostly dark buildings. Only the coffee shop, two doors down from the main intersection in downtown Wayland, showed any signs of life. I thought of walking over to get coffee, but I didn't want to leave Bob, who slept on the couch behind me.

I looked at the big lump under the quilt that my mom, who lived at a nursing home in nearby Holland, had made for him. I envied his ability to sleep. All the way home from Grand Rapids, he had stayed that way. He woke only long enough to walk up here and collapse on the couch. I was watching him while my girlfriend, Monica, was on a speaking tour.

I stayed at the window, thinking of the body sprawled in the cathedral.

Then my mind strayed to the room at Bronson Hospital, where John Blackwell had spoken to me about his wayward daughter and pleaded with me to do what I could to help find her killer. The story the retired minister—one of my former mentors—told me had been as depressing as it was unfortunate.

Listening to him that night, two days before he died, made me think of the many mistakes we all make. It reminded me of the same right now, the latest being, quite possibly, offering the reward.

I thought of Melinda—a strikingly beautiful young woman with long black hair and a slender body. We had met last year when I filled in for two months as a chaplain at Western Michigan University. A graduate student in history, she had a problem with drugs, dated the

23

wrong kinds of guys, and had a hunger to know Christ.

Just beyond my reflection in the window, I caught the first glimmers of morning, creeping down the street from the east, heralding in a Monday morning on which I would normally be asleep. Monday happened to be my only day off, and in most cases the time until noon tended to be blessedly my own.

Staring back at me in the window was a long, thin face, with hair pulled back and eyes etched underneath by hollows. On the hospital bed that night, John Blackwell gazed up at me with an intensity that even then made me very uncomfortable. He wanted from me a promise that I had been reluctant to give, but I relented. Now my choice of forging ahead with the reward—from money he had put in a bank account for me—had quite likely caused a death.

I thought for a moment that God, in his everlasting wisdom, made a big mistake when he called me to be a minister. At times, and this morning was one, I didn't know if I even believed in him. Facing life's wretchedness always made me feel this way.

Once in awhile, Christ seemed like a comic book character, a one-dimensional savior in one of those silly Sunday school books that depicted Jesus with a fake-looking beard and pearly white teeth beaming ever so kindly with a grin that made you want to get sick.

But then there was the Christ in the Garden, sweating blood before his death. This was the Christ who saved the woman from stoning; the Jesus who walked alone, tempted by Satan, in the desert, without food and full of a fear that I could taste right now. A fear of the unknown, a fear that I had failed grievously, a fear that because of me someone had died and, I suspected, more might also die before this thing got solved.

I thought again of Melinda, and of the Sunday night when I baptized her in the Rabbit River. She emerged from the water, the white baptismal gown clinging to her skin, with an angelic expression on her face. She had given herself to God. Two weeks later she was dead.

Her father had told me he thought she had come across something that had led to her death. But he didn't know what it was.

24

Thinking on all of this should have made me tired, but it didn't. I felt keyed up and needed to get out. Taking a chance that Bob would stay asleep, I went out and crossed the street for coffee.

CHAPTER FIVE

Just before I finally fell asleep about 7 a.m., Manny called, wanting me to meet him at 11 a.m. at the morgue at Blodgett Hospital in Grand Rapids. He said he and the medical examiner wanted to talk about the death in the cathedral. It was clear I had no choice in the matter, and told him I'd be there.

After two hours of fitful sleep, I got up, woke Bob, took a quick shower, put on some jeans and a sweatshirt, and then followed Bob down the steps to the parking lot.

Running late, we grabbed breakfast to go for both of us and more coffee for me at the McDonalds near the freeway. Then we headed north.

I dropped Bob off at the Hope Network jobs center on South Division where he spent his weekdays flirting with the girls and stuffing light bulbs into packages. I knew the routine, because he stayed with me every time his sister left town, which had gotten pretty frequent in the last year. In that time, she had published a book detailing her journey of faith that led to her becoming one of the first women ordained in the Christian Reformed Church. She was due back that night.

On the way to meet Manny at the morgue, I used my now recharged cell phone to call the airport to see if Monica's plane was on time. It was still supposed to be in about 8 p.m. at Gerald R. Ford International Airport.

Finally, out of breath and my head hurting from last night's adventure, I reached the basement morgue just before 11 a.m.

When I stepped inside, I saw Manny and Dr. Henry Hapwood conferring over a table on top of which lay a sheet-draped body.

"You could have started without me," I said as I entered. "It wouldn't have hurt my feelings a bit."

I'd been here before when I'd served the church downtown, both times to identify the body of parishioners. One had died drunk in the dead of winter under a freeway overpass on Bridge Street. The other, a young woman, had committed suicide.

"Long time no see, Reverend," the pathologist said, offering his hand to shake. "How are things in Wayland?'

We shook. "Busy."

Hapwood nodded at the body. "So I see."

Manny asked, "You want some coffee?" He grabbed a cup from a nearby counter and took a sip.

"I'd rather have my own."

He scowled. "That's what I meant."

"No thanks."

Soon enough, we got down to it. Hapwood wanted a blow-by-blow rundown about last night. What time did I enter the cathedral? Exactly what happened to me? Did I have any idea I was leaving behind a body when I joined Bob in the chase? Before I started, I asked if the man under the sheet was dead when we had left. Given the blood on the sidewalk, had he been killed outside and his body dumped by the altar? In a predicable move, Hapwood turned the question on me. "If so, why go to the trouble of carrying him inside? Why not leave him out there?"

I took that to mean, death occurred in the cathedral, probably. "How about a murder weapon?" I asked.

Hapwood, starting to circumvent the table, as if getting up the courage to uncover the corpse, turned my question over to Manny. Fiddling with a toothpick in the corner of his mouth, the homicide detective gave me a blank look and shrugged. But then he surprised me by actually answering my query.

The cops had found, of all things, a small, maybe 12-inch-tall, metal statue of the Blessed Mother on the bottom of the baptismal pool in the back of the church. Tendrils of blood and tissue had been identified in the holy water itself.

"He was beaten to death with a statue?"

"We're not sure."

"Do you think this man is my caller?" I asked.

"That is my hunch."

I wanted to ask why, but Hapwood began the autopsy. He removed the covering, placed it on a nearby table and then slipped a hand-held Dictaphone out of the pocket of his long white coat. I kept my attention on him, trying to ignore the naked body.

Stationed at the foot of the table, the pathologist spoke technical phrases about things he observed on the body. Manny and I stood out of his way, near a shelf carrying body parts in jars.

Hapwood noted the cold, marbled skin, blue-purple in places, especially the face. He mentioned a deep contusion on the side of the head, speculating the cause as coming from the statue recovered at the scene. Bruises circled the neck. Finally, I looked more closely.

Hands clasped over the lower abdomen, the dead man seemed to be praying. A towel had been placed over the groin area. His toes were gnarled and purplish, his shins shiny and without much hair. A thin goatee covered his chin. The long black hair lay matted underneath him.

This was not death in theory, not death in a carefully arranged casket, not an autopsy on some popular TV show, but the real deal, laid out in all its ugliness. To tell the truth, the sheer enormity of the scene was getting to me. I'd come across more than my share of blood and guts as a paramedic. I'd also been on hand for a couple of autopsies during training. But I was tired and had a pounding head this morning, and the Egg McMuffin I'd eaten for breakfast wasn't sitting right.

I closed my eyes and, for some reason, thought of the night I got the call: They'd found Melinda's body in the lake. I got out there as the ambulance hauled her away. Her face had been bloated and greenish. I had needed to step into the woods to puke.

Suddenly, I had an idea. "Manny, do you think this guy could have killed Melinda Blackwell?"

"What makes you think that?"

"Well, it is a possibility."

"I thought you said he sounded pretty broke up over her dying?"

"That doesn't mean he didn't kill her."

"If so, why come to you?"

"Out of guilt?"

"Or how about $25,000?"

He had me there.

My mind drifted, my eyes looking at anything but the body, but I paid attention again when I heard: "Captain, how about this? On the upper arm, below the shoulder. Over here."

The pathologist stood on the other side of the table and pointed. Hapwood's expression was grim as he looked at us.

We stepped over. I strained and saw a tattoo, maybe an inch tall and a half-inch wide, on the arm. The design was of a figure atop a rearing horse. The rider had an arm raised and wore a bandana on his head. Under it had been etched a famous name.

"Geronimo?" I asked.

Hapwood shrugged. "Notice, a signature, too, maybe."

Manny edged close to see. I did the same, not sure what he meant. But then I noticed two small letters, w and b, shaped in the Warner Brothers logo, at the bottom by one of the horse's hoofs.

"You think that's from the tattoo artist?" said Manny.

"If we're lucky."

The room stank of chemicals and my head felt woozy. I looked away, across the room, at those organs floating in the specimen containers.

"What do you make of that, Reverend?" asked Hapwood.

"Of what?"

"That tattoo."

My eyes went to the dead man, so dull there in the harsh light. He was displayed as if on a medical altar. He had olive skin, high cheekbones, and the long black hair. "He is an Apache?"

"Well, it would be a start. So far, we don't have much to identify

29

him by," said Hapwood.

"What about the car?" I asked Manny, thinking that would have led to a name.

"Stolen."

Feeling in need of some fresh air, I asked if he had any other questions for me. When the pathologist said not right now, I left.

Manny, however, still wanted to talk. He told me to stick around. So instead of exiting the hospital, I took a seat in the conference room down the hall, acutely aware of the sound of Hapwood sawing up the body.

Hapwood and his crew had made their mark on this space. Displayed on shelves across from me were bullets the pathologist had dug out of bodies. Some of the slugs were big and blunt, a few were in shards, and still others looked to be perfectly intact. I only knew the caliber of a couple.

On my left, part of a skeleton hung from a coat rack. Mr. Bones didn't have any legs. Piles of death reports were stacked on the floor to my right. Empty coffee cups and stale-looking donuts had been scattered at the other end of the table.

I thought of leaving, going out into the hall. The bullets and the skeleton bugged me. But I stayed, my attention drifting to that pile of reports, a dozen folders, most fairly thick. I thought of looking through them, but had no reason.

Instead, I bowed my head, started to pray and kept at it, asking the Lord's help to beat back a sadness that felt almost overwhelming. In the middle of praying, though, my brain started to calm. My thoughts flat-lined and I had an inspiration. I thought of Preacher.

Preacher was a one-time street person whom I'd helped out in a variety of ways over the years. He had attended my church in downtown Grand Rapids and frequently rolled through my office door in his wheelchair to talk. He also had been a tattoo artist, and, in fact, had owned a pretty big shop before he lost it for back taxes. He still did some tattoo work, although he mainly tended bar at a West Side bowling alley.

I glanced up as the door swung open and Manny and the good doctor appeared. Both gave me a funny glance, as if they had seen something on my face.

Needing a caffeine fix, they headed for the coffee pot. Hapwood poured out the old grounds, stuck in some new ones and fired up the Mr. Coffee.

Manny meanwhile went for a box of fresh donuts I hadn't noticed. He bit into a chocolate-covered one. I watched as he ate it and then went for another. Once he finished the second one, he hit me with a question that caught me off guard. "Turkstra, you're good pals with Preacher aren't you?"

I couldn't help shaking my head in surprise.

"What?" asked Manny.

"I don't know if this is good or not, but I was thinking about him, too."

Pins crashed and fell. Preacher waited to make sure they all fell before turning his specially rigged wheelchair our way. A crafty smile cut across his face. We were at the bowling alley on West Leonard Street where he worked. "Mark that one a strike for the Gipper,'" he said to Manny, the scorekeeper.

Manny had ordered and eaten a hamburger from the bar. Now keeping track of Preacher's progress, he shook his head, not happy playing a secondary role here.

The cop was hoping, as well as I, that this guy who lost his legs many years ago, maybe in Vietnam and maybe not, could be of help.

"How am I doing, Captain Manny, my man?" Preacher asked, reaching down as his ball popped out of the chute.

"Roll the ball, Preacher."

Preacher got his nickname from how he liked to talk up a storm, on many topics, including God, when he got drunk. Now a bartender at this bowling alley, he had taken a break when we stopped in. But he didn't want to sit. He needed to get in some practice for a handicapped team he was on. In our group of three, he was the only one bowling.

31

Preacher was a marvel to watch, as he spun in his chair, shot for the alley and then let it fly.

Not nearly as impressed as me, Manny yawned, using the back of his hand to rub his eyes. On the way out of the hospital, he suggested I tag along, partly so he could ask questions, but partly, I knew, because Preacher didn't fancy cops, and Manny probably figured he'd be a little more willing to talk with me here. On the way, Rodriguez had called someone in the vice squad, and that person agreed Preacher might be of help. That person, I took to be another detective, promised to start going through the computer to see what they had on other local tattoo artists.

We watched Preacher's ball tumble hard and straight, smashing the head pin. But the five and six were left standing.

Preacher whipped around, facing us and swore.

"Take a load off, so we can talk. I've got a real job to do," said Manny, scratching on the sheet. He then checked his beeper, glowered and stuck it away.

Preacher wore a cut-off sweatshirt emblazoned with an alligator in sunglasses, jeans wrapped around his stubs and fingerless gloves on both hands. "What's the rush, Gus?"

"Believe it or not, I'm trying to solve a murder." Manny leaned back in the plastic chair, his weary face all business.

Preacher smiled, showing a gap or two in his teeth. "Well, you've come to the right place, Ace."

"What do you know about tattoo artists in town?" I asked.

"They're all amateurs. Unlike yours truly—the one-man tattooing machine, at one time that is."

Manny stood, dropping the pencil on the score sheet. "I've got a call to make."

We watched him shamble off.

I tried to get comfortable on the hard, scoop-seated bench, hearing the grind of pin-setting machines and rumble of balls on shiny wood. "This is important," I said to Preacher.

Manny leaned on a wall by the bar, talking on the pay phone, a finger in one ear.

Preacher asked why we wanted to know about tattoos.

"Like he said, it might have to do with a murder."

"Who died?"

I wasn't sure how much to tell him, but need not have worried.

"This has to do with that stiff in the Catholic church?" he asked.

I filled him in, focusing on the tattoo of the outlaw Indian.

Preacher found that pretty interesting and asked a question. "This tattoo had the Warner Brothers deal at the bottom?"

I nodded.

He thought it over. "That might be Wooly Bully's. WB's how he does it. Specializes in cartoons, devils and, like, Greek god figures. His real name's Russ Woods."

"Do you know him?"

"Who don't?"

"Where can we find him?"

Preacher didn't answer. Instead, he grabbed the wheels of his chair and swiveled around toward the lane. Balls thudded on other lanes.

I watched him bowl another couple of frames. After making a spare, he turned to me, rolled close and, making sure no one else was in hearing range, asked: "Are we talking here about some of that loot you're offering?"

"Loot?"

"You know that reward you been talking about on TV."

"I thought we were friends?"

"Hey, Rev, don't kill a guy for asking." He eyed me seriously. "I mean, hey, man, you're all over the place talking about that reward, and, well, why not, if I can help?"

My announcement had gotten pretty wide play. Now I regretted all of the coverage I had worked so hard to generate.

"Look, Rev, if it helps, I won't take all of the money if my info solves the caper. Just a fair percentage," said Preacher.

"Whatever."

"If you don't mind me asking, where'd you get that kind of cash?"

"I can't say."

"Can't or won't?"

"Both."

Manny showed up, holding a couple of Cokes.

"Hey, Captain, me and Turkstra been busy working on that murder for you," said Preacher, fiddling with his ball.

Manny shot me a look over his raised pop can.

"He thinks he knows that tattoo guy," I said.

This brightened the cop's mood, especially when I gave him the name. "Where does he work?" Manny asked.

"Last I knew, it was on South Division some place."

Manny handed me a Coke, then stepped away to check his beeper again.

I gave Preacher the hard eye, trying to get him to cough up more on Russ Woods.

"Now he might be over there on Stocking, by the old Kopper Top." He meant a bar, not too far away.

"This place have a name?" I asked.

"Not sure."

Manny gave me a look that said let's hit it.

But we stayed for a moment to watch Preacher turn his chair, position his ball at his side and concentrate on the pins. Then, with one hand he spun the chair forward, somehow keeping it straight, and with the other arced back with the ball. Just as his arm flashed forward, Manny called: "Hey, smart guy, you're shoes are untied."

Cussing up a storm, Preacher dropped a gutter ball just as we left.

CHAPTER SIX

DJ's Tattoo and Body Works sat between a second-hand clothes store and an adults-only movie theater. The large, airbrushed mural of a nearly bare-breasted woman with her blue hair on fire filled the front window of the building.

Manny pulled to the curb, got on his radio to tell the dispatcher his location, and then told me he'd be right back.

When I said I'm coming, too, Rodriguez surprised me by not pitching a fit. He even held the door open and let me go first into the cramped lobby showing walls covered with stencils and replicas of tattoos. I saw a big variety to choose from. One especially struck me. It showed Christ riding a Harley.

Rodriguez rang a bell on a small counter next to a tropical fish tank, trying to stir up some response. The cop palmed the bell three more times before a voice called from beyond a doorway decorated with long strings of beads, telling us to come back. A few moments later, we stepped into a small, carpeted room that had posters of Jim Morrison, Elvis and Cary Grant pasted to the walls.

A cat shot out from under the table where a ratty looking tattoo artist worked on a woman's back.

I vaguely recalled the tattoo parlor along the beach in San Diego that I stumbled into with a couple Navy submariner buddies, just before our sub shoved off for a six-month tour of the South China Sea. Never much of a drinker, I was drunk that time and had a guy tattoo, of all things, an anchor on my lower back. My dinky nautical symbol paled in comparison to the tattoo possibilities on the walls in the lobby, as well as those covering the broad back of the woman on whom the long-haired, tattoo artist drew with his ink gun.

"Sorry, no one was out front, but Dezi here is my gal Friday and she's a little bit busy right now," said the guy, jabbing the gun between the woman's shoulder blades, etching in what looked like teardrops.

"We're looking for Wooly Bully," Manny said.

The guy with the tattoo gun craned his head in our direction. "And who might you two be?"

Manny showed him his badge. I took a spot against a wall, keeping an eye out for that cat.

"So," said Manny, "are you him or not?"

The tattoo artist's demeanor hardened. Nodding, he went back to his work, waiting for Manny to get down to it.

After looking at his beeper and flipping through numbers, Manny did just that. "I hear you specialize in tattooing Indians and cowboys, devils, unusual stuff?"

Wooly Bully kept working. "I draw lots of things," he answered after a few seconds, running the tip of his gun in the hollows of the woman's spine.

Rodriguez stepped close and grabbed Wooly's wrist. "Yes or no?"

Wooly gently extricated himself from the cop and stepped to the side. He then grabbed and toked on a dead stogie that had been sitting in an ashtray next to a lava lamp. "What's this about?"

Rodriguez slipped Polaroid photos out of the pocket of his shirt. I'd already seen them. One showed a long view of the guy with the bashed-in head, made that way by of all things a statute of Christ's mother. Another was a close-up of the face. A third showed the Indian on the horse. Bully took and held them close, slit an eye to get a better view.

"Is that your logo at the bottom?" prodded the cop.

Wooly held them up, looking genuinely interested then perplexed. "Hey, Dez, take a look. See if you're thinking what I'm thinking."

His receptionist turned and hefted herself to a sitting position, holding a towel to her breasts, and took the pictures from her boss.

She had tattoos on her shoulders, one showing a unicorn/dragon combo and the other a mixture of designs.

She shuffled through the pictures, making faces, as if to say these were gross. After awhile, she turned to Bully. "It might've been from the DeltaPlex."

The DeltaPlex was a huge, former indoor ice rink and arena that once housed local semi-pro teams. Now, the place played host to pro wrestling matches, heavy metal and rap concerts, gun shows and, I gathered, tattoo conventions.

Manny asked when this was, and Bully answered last year sometime.

"How can you be sure?"

"That's the first Geronimo I've done."

"Do you keep records on the names?" Manny asked.

"Not really."

Dezi shifted slightly, still holding the photos. Just above her, Jim Morrison lay in a tub of bubbly water, a slight halo over his head, eyes impish and desperate at the same time. I wondered if he and Cary and Elvis were in the same heaven, or hell. Finally, Wooly's gal Friday put the pictures in her lap and gazed curiously at me. It was clear that the towel clasped to her chest was all that existed between her upper body and the outside world. I tried not to stare at her breasts, barely covered by the cloth. "You're the minister's friend, aren't you?" she said to me.

I think I blushed. "Pardon?"

"Reverend Smit, isn't it? The one who wrote the book."

She meant the memoir that Monica had written describing her life leading up to being ordained in our small denomination. Even though Monica had gotten quite a bit of publicity from the book, Dezi surprised me by the comment.

I told her I was, wondering, though, how she put me together with Monica.

Bully smoked, watching her with mild interest. She lifted her nose, daring him to give her a hard time. Inside the extra pounds I saw a girl whose features bordered on pretty. Her legs, also laced with body art, hung off the table and looked plump and curvy. Her eyes held an inner light that may have come from pills. I saw in her face an odd mixture of suffering and playfulness. "I took her class. The one on, what do you call it, empowerment, at community ed," she explained. "And you picked her up sometimes."

"Really?"

"Yup."

Monica taught the course at night through the public schools. A couple times I'd sat in the back, waiting to take her home, and was always impressed with the connection she made with the women. She would go from desk to desk, quietly talking, a hand on a shoulder, checking work she had assigned. When she lectured, she did it with obvious passion. I didn't recall ever seeing this Dezi in the class.

"Dezi's a budding woman's libber," Bully told me.

"Kiss it," she snapped at him.

Bully shrugged, still smoking. Dezi flipped through the photos again.

"Do you recognize him?" I asked her.

Dezi's eyes slid in Bully's direction, and then turned to me, as if she knew more than she was saying.

Glowering at his beeper, Manny asked if Bully had a phone. The tattoo artist led him out and down the hall.

Left alone with Dezi, she got even chummier. "Aren't you the one offering the reward about that girl that died?" she asked. "Like you were on TV, right?"

"Guilty again."

Dezi's face grew serious. "And, like, weren't you the one who was in the church last night where they found that body?"

"I was on the news?"

"TV."

Again she surprised me. She didn't strike me as a news junkie.

Dezi gazed at the photos again. "Is this the man in the church? Is that why you're here?"

"It is."

"Did he want the reward?" she asked.

I shrugged. "You follow things pretty closely."

She smiled.

"What's this about a reward?" Bully asked, returning.

Dezi looked at him with a wary expression. "About a girl who was killed a few weeks ago."

"What girl?"

"Wasn't she Indian or something?" Dezi asked me.

"Partly."

"Why did she get killed?"

"The police are trying to find that out."

Wooly looked at her and then at me and sighed. "The cop wants you to go through the books," he said to Dezi.

"Me?"

"You're the bookkeeper, sweetheart."

"Like hell," she shot back.

Bully broke into a big grin. "Now don't go getting mouthy on me now."

Dezi shrank back, as if he might hit her. I watched him keenly, thinking that he reminded me of a ferret.

Meanwhile, though, Manny returned and told me to get lost. He wanted to talk to Wooly Bully and the girl alone.

CHAPTER SEVEN

Although he's rarely around to use it, Kent County's airport is named after former President Jerry Ford. Most flights in and out of it are puddle jumpers to larger airports that can take you on to your destination. But don't get me wrong, ours can be a hopping place, as it was on this Monday evening.

Bob had his face pressed to the large window, watching planes taxi in and out. Just about dusk, the sky looked soft in the west. Darkness, though, had fallen in the east, and it's out of that black blanket that Monica's plane should soon be descending.

My own reflection, showing above Bob's head, looked a little hollow, my hair stringy, tied in the back with a rubber band, my mouth tight. I couldn't see my lump from the cathedral, but it still felt tender.

To tell the truth, old Truman (my middle name, inspired by Harry Truman,) looked pretty wiped out, and add to that anxious as well.

Not long before, I'd spoken on the pay phone to Monica, who had me paged to give me the skinny on her slightly delayed flight out of Chicago. She was now coming in just before nine. I had told her that was fine, but then asked if she minded if we made a quick stop on the way home at the Orbit Room, where my newfound friend Dezi asked to meet. The tattooed lady had joined me in the lobby a few minutes after Manny kicked me out.

We talked and she told me the books and receipts they kept were useless, and that for various reasons she wanted nothing to do with helping the cops anyhow. But she might be able to help me, for a piece of the reward, identify the guy with the Indian tattoo.

I'm not sure why Dezi wanted to meet at the Orbit Room, but I decided to bring Monica along in hopes that as Dezi's former teacher she might be of help. The dance place happened to be on the way to Monica's condo anyhow. As for Manny, I didn't tell him about the meeting.

Bob now stood, nearly bumping into me, and smacked his palm on the airport window. On the far end of the runway, lights dropped quickly from the sky and wheels rushed onto the pavement.

Not long after, the loudspeaker announced the arrival from O'Hare.

We watched the Northwest flight into the gate. Given all the new restrictions at airports since the 9/11 attacks, we had to wait in this area beyond the security check.

Bob spit on his hand and wiped it over his flat head, slicking down a few stray strands of black hair. He wore his vintage Goodwill wool sport coat, the same one he slipped on for important occasions, as well as polo shirt and the venerable Green Bay Packers warm-up pants. As usual, the side pockets of his pants bulged with debris.

Butterflies began to battle in my belly. Monica and I had been through so much together and were once again treading across thin ice as her new ministry took off and I continued to do my ministry in the small town. I'd wanted to cement things between us, but she had been pulled in another direction. Then again, so had I.

A fair-sized group of people waited for the passengers from the flight to deplane. Bob pushed his way through to get to the front, just this side of the metal detectors. I hung back, able to see over most heads.

Always this scene—people arriving, if even from a short business trip—struck me with its drama. Friends and families embraced, cried, happy to see one another. This went on as Bob bounced on his toes at the front, waiting for his older sister.

Finally, she showed—a small, stylishly dressed blonde woman with large green eyes, walking down the ramp, emerging from another world, a sought-after preacher and author, scanning the crowd for a familiar face. She couldn't miss Bob. He was doing jumping

41

jacks. Monica smiled brightly when she saw him. Her grin dimmed a watt or two when she spotted me moving her way. I wondered if she was having second thoughts about the Orbit Room.

A few seconds later, Bob had her in a hug and I was at her side, grabbing for her carry-on and bending down to catch a kiss.

Soon, we strode toward baggage claim. Bob went ahead, flicking a thumb at framed pictures of local sites on the walls.

Monica and I did the usual—how was your flight, did we mind waiting, and so on until we reached the twirling carousel on which bags had not yet been dumped. Even then, though, we tried to keep it light. As we spoke about the little things, I saw a glow and beauty to her that felt compelling and disturbing at the same time.

But I also noticed the weariness of many miles etched on her face. There was puffiness as well. "Are you sure you don't mind stopping?" I asked finally.

"It's on the way."

Bob blundered up, carrying a large green suitcase bearing international tags. He had gotten it right.

Monica stood a head smaller than me. Her hair, cut short and lightly spiked, made her look younger than her actual age—38. She wore a silk scarf around her neck and silver studs for earrings. I imagined her in Amsterdam preaching up a storm, her words on fire for the Lord. Now that she was back, she'd have little rest before headlining a big ecumenical event at the downtown convention center—an event that she had mentioned when we spoke on the phone earlier. It was a very big deal for her, but I had forgotten about it.

"You know, Cal," she now said, "I'm not so sure I know Dezi."

I gave a description, highlighting the body art.

Monica mulled it over and smiled. "Oh yes, the born-again topless dancer."

"I thought she worked at the tattoo place?"

"They call it moonlighting."

"You remember her?"

"I think so."

As we walked out of the terminal, she turned to me and asked, "Calvin, are you sure you want me to go with you?"

"Why?"

She stopped. We stood on the walkway outside the terminal. "I don't know. You're involved again in a murder and ..."

I waited. When she didn't respond, I asked, "And?"

She rubbed a knuckle in one eye and watched as Bob hailed a cab that we didn't need. "And ... nothing. "

I didn't push it. We stepped off the curb. I waved the waiting cabbie away and then followed Monica and her brother into Short-Term Parking.

CHAPTER EIGHT

The Orbit Room, a former movie theater, sat next to a topless joint called Sensations. The neon outline of a naked woman pulsed on a sign at the entrance to the strip club.

Maybe a year before Monica led a march outside the club, protesting the way in which the owners treated the dancers. Actually, it was a little incredible to see some liberal church people, taking to the streets to highlight the cause of bad labor relations between the strip-tease dancers and management. But it sure got news coverage, and didn't hurt sales of Monica's book any.

Monica stared out the window of my truck, looking glum, as I pulled into a parking spot near Sensations. Bob hummed the "Mission Impossible" theme song.

Before we got out, Monica turned to me and asked, "Did you see this man's body?"

"Under a blanket when they brought him out."

She rubbed her eyes and shook her head.

"What?"

"I'm not sure how you keep getting involved in these things, Calvin."

This had not been the first time that murder had ensnared me. Gazing at her, the pink light from the nearby Sensations signs flashing into my truck and across her face, I felt a slight trembling guilt. She'd had very long plane ride and now I dragged her here. "How about if I take you home?"

"I'm OK."

Behind us, Bob started in on the old Herman's Hermit tune, "I'm Henry the Eighth, I Am."

"You know, really, I know that you're tired."

She gave me a quick, tired smile. "Thanks. I'm OK. If it can somehow help the police with this case."

We got soft drinks and sat down just as the band, The Slit-Eyed Lizards, finished beating down the walls with a sound that made my head hurt.

Our table rimmed the packed dance floor. Most of those in the crowd looked to be in their late teens or early twenties. They bounced and gyrated, swinging their hips at one another. I wondered if any of them were Christians, thinking that you could never tell these days.

Disco balls strung from the ceiling caught light and sent it everywhere. Above and behind us hung a balcony on which were arranged more tables.

I scanned the room for Dezi, but didn't see her.

After a couple minutes, Monica said she was going to find a phone and check her messages at church. She looked even more tired than before.

Sitting across from me, Bob smacked his hands on the tabletop. "Are you glad to see your sister?" I asked.

"You silly rabbit." A smile played on his pudding face. His polo shirt showed an emblem of the comic book character Silver Surfer on the front. The Surfer looked like an off-color Oscar statue with anorexia. Bob liked being out this late at night.

"You want more to drink?" I asked.

He looked into his empty glass, cupped it in his large hands. "Deputy Dawg," he replied.

"What's with the cartoons?"

He eyed me seriously, but didn't answer.

We watched the kids dance. Some wore rings, studs and jewelry in their ears, noses and eyebrows. One girl near us wiggled her tongue, revealing three silver flashes. I still didn't see a pudgy woman with tattoos.

Then out of the corner of my eye, I caught two women headed our way, Monica and Dezi, as the next group tuned up on stage.

45

"Look who found me," said Monica.

Dezi pulled up next to Bob. She wore a huge white T-shirt, which said, "If I'm a bitch, a man made me that way." Dark stirrup pants stuck to her legs like paint. Her cheeks glistened. I took her to be in her mid to late twenties, a few years older than most of the people on the dance floor. "Who's the hunk?" she asked, placing her on hand on Bob's shoulder, apparently not referring to me.

"Spawn," he replied, "unstoppable creature from the deep."

"What's his name really?" asked Dezi.

Monica told her.

"Keep the power burning," Bob interjected, sticking a fist to his mouth.

Dezi laughed. "This guy's a riot."

"Nice T-shirt," I said.

She stretched it out. "You like it?"

"What's not to like?"

After Monica sat, Dezi grabbed a chair and slid close to Bob, making eye contact. Bob hung his head, shy. "Cat got your tongue, big guy?" she asked.

"Anything important on the answering machine?" I wondered of Monica.

"Nothing that can't wait."

I felt the chill deepening between us. Unable to figure what to say, we both watched Dezi, the tattooed man-hater, flirt with Bob. Then Monica and Dezi reminisced a bit about the empowerment class.

Meanwhile, four young men with turned-around baseball caps on their heads got ready to play. They wore loose shirts, baggy beach-bum shorts and sandals. "These guys really crank," Dezi said to Bob. Then she turned to me. "They're not rappers, though." She said it as if I would think of that as a bad thing.

Monica's brother, looking at the table, twisted on the sides of his glass. "Talk to me, Dezi," I said.

One of the beach bums strummed his guitar, making me think of fingernails on a blackboard, only amplified. "Dezi?" I urged. "You

46

said you might be able to help."

Without looking at me, she said, "I'm working on it."

"Do you have a name?" I asked.

Dezi shrugged. In the hazy purple-tinted light, her face looked doll-like, fragile, easily broken, and yet harsh. She leaned back, looking at me through half-closed eyes. "I called a friend who might know, like, know someone in Detroit. Maybe a relative."

"Can you tell me anything about that tattoo. Did it have any significance?"

"Are you going to tell that cop we talked?"

"Probably."

She didn't like this, turning her attention to the crowd for a minute or so. And then, as if pulled by invisible strings, she and Bob got up at the same time. Dezi started to grab his hand to lead him toward the dance floor. "C'mon, Dezi," I yelled over the music. "Are you going help or not!"

Monica looked startled by my anger. But I didn't care.

Dezi dragged Bob into the crowd, where dancers flung themselves into one another, bodies slamming bodies, as if seeing who would break first.

For a moment, the crowd parted and I watched Dezi talking into the same ear she'd been fondling. Then she started swiveling her feet, arms over her head, her breasts swaying inside the feminist T-shirt. Bob did nothing for a few seconds before beginning to move as well—slow, jerky, his legs and arms stiff, but he was trying, to a kind of techno swing beat. Definitely the Orbit Room offered a mix of music styles.

I watched half-heartedly, wondering what to do next.

The next song or two weren't too bad, and the body slamming ceased. As a sort of slow one started, I turned to Monica and asked if she wanted to dance.

"No thanks."

So we sat.

As we did, I thought about us.

For the better part of a decade we'd warily circled and closed in on one another. We'd dated, broken up, come back together, and currently we languished in another limbo period. Don't let anyone say ministers can't be confused. I hated to consider what God, or our congregations, thought of our waffling. We were both acutely aware of the thin line we walked.

We had met when I was working at a storefront church in Chicago. She came in to interview homeless people for a paper she was doing for a class at the University of Chicago Divinity School.

As the music built and flowed and dancers clung to one another, I thought about New York.

She had gone there to address the Christian Booksellers Convention, and I took time off to tag along. It had been a wonderful long weekend—maybe too wonderful. We had separate rooms, and then one night …

The body slamming began again, and Dezi appeared at the table with Bob. "Hey, why don't you two give it a try," she said.

I turned to Monica. She was yawning. It was time to go. But before I could get up, I felt a vibration in my pocket. It was my cell phone. Because of the din, I had to take the call in the bathroom.

Not too long after the call, I was on the road. Alone.

CHAPTER NINE

Norbert Nash gazed out a window, one hand clasped behind his back, the other holding a cigarette, as I stepped into his large, book-lined office on the top floor of the diocesan center. I saw his somber reflection in the glass.

"Reverend Turkstra," he said, turning quickly, as if I'd caught him daydreaming. Or maybe he was embarrassed I'd seen him smoking. He leaned over to a table near the widow and crushed out his cigarette in an ashtray, next to which sat a small pile of books and a long, slender, modern statue of Christ.

Barry Lazio stepped in behind me, smelling of cologne and cigarettes. He had met me at the front entrance and, apologizing profusely for calling so late to ask me here, led me to the office of the chancellor of the local Catholic diocese.

Nash's soft, vaguely sad-looking eyes settled on me. He had a small, tight mouth and darkish features. We had met a few times. I knew him to be a tough money guy. "Would you like something to drink? Soda, coffee?" he asked.

"Nothing."

He nodded grimly. "If you don't mind, I'm going to have something to settle my stomach," Nash said, a hand resting on his belly. Although he was a large man, there was also a certain delicacy to him.

A signal of some sort passed between him and Barry, and the mayor slipped out.

Nash and I then faced each other over 15 feet of thick purple-blue carpet. A high plaster ceiling rose over us. Recessed light cast oblong shadows in the far corners of the room.

He had curly gray-black hair and a broad forehead. In his early sixties, he looked tired. Beyond him, out the window, I saw the lights of cars driving along Burton Street in front of the diocesan center. The dance club was to the south, in another dimension. When I'd told Monica the mayor had called and what he wanted, she wasn't too happy. And I didn't blame her. As it turned out, Dezi had a friend with a car and offered to drive Monica and Bob home. But I insisted that Monica and Bob ride with me, it being the least I could do.

On the short drive to Monica's condo, we didn't speak. Pulling up to her place and then carrying in her bags, I kept hoping she would invite me back when I had finished, but she didn't. She gave me a quick hug and a cool kiss and told me thanks for watching Bob, who by then had turned on the TV, and that she would talk to me tomorrow.

"Have a seat," said the chancellor.

He sank in the seat behind his desk. I took the chair in front of him.

Nash's black suit looked pouched and wrinkled. Around his neck he wore a tie that matched the pale yellow color of his shirt. He thanked me again for coming, and then said: "I know it's late and you've been very busy."

"How can I help?"

Nash picked up a pen and started to doodle on a pad in front of him. Barry had offered nothing about the purpose of this meeting, other than to say it had to do with the guy whose body turned up in the cathedral.

Finally, the chancellor said, "The diocese is very troubled by what happened last night. I'm sure you can understand that." There was a faint, singsong accent in his voice.

"Of course."

"It must have been quite an ordeal for you."

"More so for the victim," I said.

Nash winced and nodded.

"What is it that you want, sir?" I asked.

"I'm hoping you can tell me what happened in there, from your perspective, of course," he said. "I want to understand it better, if that's even possible… And then I want to talk to you about another matter." When he finished, he smiled weakly.

"What other matter?"

He held up a hand, as if warning me to slow down. "I'm hoping we can help each other."

So I sketched what had gone down. When I finished, he asked a few questions. He seemed surprised that the murder weapon was a statue of the Blessed Mother.

After knocking on the door, Lazio stepped in. He stuck a tall glass of what I took to be milk on a blotter before Nash, and then took a can of Diet Pepsi and sat in an easy chair on my right. He wore a black leather jacket over a purple turtleneck and stretched his legs in front of him. His face was flushed. His hair was slicked back, Mafioso-style.

Nash meanwhile stared glumly at his milk, as if expecting some-thing bad—like a cockroach or worm—to pop to the top.

Barry sipped his Pepsi.

Leaving the milk sit, Nash said, "Barry, Reverend Turkstra says the murder weapon was a statue of the Holy Mother. Did you know that?"

Actually, he said, he did know.

"Was that in the news?"

"I forgot to bring it up, Norb," said the mayor.

Nash's hand clasped his tie, just below the knot around his neck. "Where, dear God, did the statue come from? Was it ours?"

"The sacristy."

"I wish you would have told me."

"Sorry."

An awkward silence stretched between us, until the chancellor raised his glass and said: "Pray God, we find out who did this." Then he drank.

Downing the milk seemed to be a signal for the real reason for the meeting to surface. "Reverend, there's something that the mayor told me and we agreed we wanted to talk to you about it—and tonight, if possible."

The real reason they wanted to talk, I soon learned, came down to money. In many ways it always did—look at Dezi and, for that matter, Preacher, and, let's not leave out, my dead friend in the cathedral. All of them asked about the money.

Anyhow, an anonymous donor, Barry Lazio told me, wanted to add another $30,000 to the reward fund, either for an ID on the man who died in the cathedral or for Melinda Blackwell, but preferably both.

That was a chunk of change, no doubt an amount that would bring more information—and possibly trouble—out of the woodwork. "Do you really think more money is going to do it?" I asked.

"Do you?" Nash asked.

"It could backfire, like last night."

"Do you see that as your fault, Reverend?"

"Without a reward, he wouldn't have called."

We were silent a few moments. "Who is the anonymous donor?" I asked.

Settled back in his chair in front of his milk-stained glass, Nash didn't answer at first. His face looked reflective. Then he told me that he couldn't say one way or another. That's how the donor wanted it.

When I asked him why, he pitched it back to Barry who, looking apologetic, said, "Neither the donor nor we want the publicity. But, for that matter, Calvin, you've never said where the $25,000 had come from."

He had me there. So I told him. "It came from Melinda's father."

As another silence arose, I could tell by the chancellor's expression that he was looking for my response to the offer.

I thought how mad the cops would be if I announced an additional reward. Look at the mess the money caused already. For another thing, I didn't like to be the messenger boy for some anonymous donor. Still, if money was what it took, then why not give it a shot? I was in this far enough. There was no turning back now. I did make a final pitch, though, for full disclosure.

"Why doesn't the diocese make the offer itself—or we do it together in a press conference? It might even have that much more impact, the diocese getting involved. This donor doesn't have to be mentioned."

Nash didn't buy it. The diocese had to stay in the shadows. Was I up for it or not?

"Can you tell me why this donor is willing to be so generous?" I asked.

"Because, Reverend, he wants to see justice done, just like you."

Twenty minutes later, Barry and I stood side by side in the parking lot behind the chancery office—a sturdy brick building used for many years as the seminary. As numbers of priest in training had diminished, the large structure had been emptied of classrooms and dorms and church offices took over. I'd been here a time or two to meet with the human development people who brought refugees into town and linked them with area churches.

Big pines towered above us. Beyond the large, sheltering branches spread a soft salting of stars. Barry's shiny red BMW was parked by the front entrance that we had just exited.

A check for $30,000 would be deposited tomorrow in the account whose number I had given Nash.

On the way down from the chancellor's office, neither Barry nor I had spoken. Now he was dragging on a cigarette, gazing across a darkened baseball field at the neighborhood across the way. His face was obscured by the shadows cast down by the tree branches. I saw the tip of his cigarette flare, and then it flew away and fell to the ground in a shower of sparks. "Thanks for agreeing, Calvin."

Looking at him, I thought back to last night and of a couple of things that had been bugging me.

"I wonder why that side door to the cathedral was open," I said. "Any ideas?"

"Kroger told me he thinks the people from the AA meeting left it open."

He told me AA met in the cathedral on Sunday nights. "Did anyone from AA see anything? Have they asked them?" I wondered.

"I think the police have, and someone told them that they think the dead guy was in the meeting for awhile, but then left before it ended."

"Kroger tell you this, too?"

"He does work for the city, Calvin."

I wondered what else he had heard. "You say the statue of Mary was from the sacristy? Was it locked up?"

"No, it was out in the open."

"That makes me think maybe this is someone who is familiar with the church. Maybe someone from AA?"

Lazio shook his head. "I wish the hell we knew, Calvin. You can't believe how terrible I feel about this. For that man, for the church. It's a tragedy."

"You've been a member of the cathedral for a long time, haven't you?" I asked, just recalling this fact.

"Yes, I love that place. To have God's house desecrated like that is hard to take."

Barry walked me to my truck, where we stood. He looked as if he had more to say. I could smell his cologne.

Lazio stared hard at me, as if what he was about to say was tougher for him to ask than for me to answer. "What do you think that man wanted to tell you, Calvin? "

I looked to the sky, where distant stars flickered so many millions of miles away amid clouds of gas and black holes and dark energy we couldn't see but knew existed. The universe was a vast, unfolding mystery, but so was this world and what we did in it. And yet, we could make guesses, shape approximations, and basically have faith that we could eventually find our way through the confusing dark.

"I wish I knew."

"I hear it might have had to do with some kind of map."

I perked up. "What? Who told you this?"

Barry shook his head, eyeing me carefully. "I can't say."

This was very important, and freely offered. I wondered as much about this so-called map, as to why he was telling me this. "Map to what?"

"Possibly to a buried document."

"Are you sure of that?" I asked.

"It's what I hear."

My eyes turned again to those stars, to that huge milky mystery. "I don't get it."

"Look, Calvin." I felt his hand on my arm. "We need to get the additional reward out. We need to find it, before anyone else."

"Find what?"

Lazio stepped away, deeper into the shadows. "The map. What I hear is it could turn the casino deal upside down."

Now he had me. But he wouldn't say anything else. "Barry! What map! How could it affect the casino?"

He meant, of course, the casino that Indians in Gun Lake, but not many from my church, wanted to build south of Wayland near the expressway. I now tried to recall a snatch of conversation from last night. The guy with the Geronimo tattoo had mumbled something about a fight over something Melinda had. I wanted to bring back the exact words, but couldn't.

"Barry, what about the map and the casino?"

"Look, Calvin, you know as well as me that it is all starting to come down to one thing."

"What thing?"

"Does the tribe really own that land where they want to build? Is it really where the tribe lived 150 years ago?"

Truthfully, the issue has been so complicated that I had found it hard to follow. It seemed someone—interests in Grand Rapids or in Wayland—was filing law suits every month.

"Barry, are you saying that this map, if that's what it is, gives a location for tribal property?"

He shrugged, eyeing me closely. "Think about it, Calvin. Some very bad stuff has gone down here."

"Over a map?"

When his cell phone rang, he told me he had to take the call. He suggested we could talk later.

"How do you know this, Barry?"

"Let's talk later."

I wanted to wait, but he wouldn't have it. He put a hand over his phone. "Calvin, promise me if you hear anything, anything at all about a map that you'll get back to me."

I stepped closer to him, smelling pine all around us. "Barry, you need to come a lot cleaner with me than you are."

"I will, but not now. Tomorrow. We'll talk tomorrow."

CHAPTER TEN

The first thing the next morning I made coffee and toasted two bagels, piled on the peanut butter, and headed, breakfast in tow, for my truck and the two-mile trip to my church. By the time I ate my bagels, sipped down half of the coffee and had listened to a couple of Beatles songs on the tape deck, I arrived. I did my best to keep my mind off the murder and instead on my church duties.

A white clapboard structure first built by the Methodists in the 1870s, Wayland Township Community Church sat among farm fields along a county road south and east of town.

I parked in the gravel lot and walked up the creaking wood steps to the side door that led into the back of the sanctuary and to my office in the very rear. I cranked on the space heater under my desk, pulled the blinds so I could look out at acres of wilting summer corn stalks and, trying to keep my mind clear, prayed.

Before I set down to church business, I called Monica, first at her apartment, where I only got the answering machine, and also at church, where they said she was in a meeting. I left messages at both places.

Moving along, I tried DJ's Body Works, where another machine was my only option if I wanted to leave a message for Dezi. Letting her know that I was able to up the ante, given the anonymous donation, might convince her to deliver.

Then I called the mayor's office, only to run head-on into a secretary who told me he had meetings all morning, and refused to give me his cell number. I needed to follow up with him on his comments. What he had said about a map made me toss and turn all night.

Not sure if I should, I nonetheless called the Grand Rapids Press and got in touch with Randy VanderMolen, the religion editor. I told him I had an announcement to make. Should I give it to him, or Joe Casey, the cop reporter?

"You can give it me, but I want to talk to you anyway about something else."

"What's that?"

"A rumor we're hearing."

"Which is?"

He didn't answer. He said he had an important interview he had to do. We set a time to talk later. Hanging up, I wondered what rumor he meant.

I had the sense of things heating up, of matters tugging at me and pulling me in directions I didn't want to take.

I needed to get my mind on my job. As best I could, I shoved everything else aside and started in on research for my Sunday sermon.

Then the phone rang. I grabbed it and found Benny Plasterman, the Barry County undersheriff and a good friend, on the other end. We spent a minute or two on small talk, and then he asked me about what happened at the cathedral. Gun Lake, where they found Melinda's body, was in Barry County. Benny had two detectives still trying to sort through leads, cold as they had become, on Melinda's murder. Since both were out of town on business, Benny had told them he would talk to me.

After I filled him in about the other night, I mentioned my meeting with the mayor and the chancellor. I mentioned the additional reward money, which led to a discussion about the wisdom of making a big news splash about it, and then—if for no other reason than to change the subject—I asked about a map. I decided to tell him that the mayor had mentioned it to me.

Benny paused, and I pressed, and he paused again. "Hang on a second," he said finally.

I could hear papers rustling on the other end of the line. "OK, there's something in here in the investigation report about that, yes."

"There is?"

"Yes."

"Is this public knowledge? I've never heard of this before."

"Looking at it here, Cal, it is in a supplemental. It's new."

"And it says what?"

Benny paused again. "Cal, I'm sorry, but I better talk to my guys before telling you much more."

"But, Lazio knows about it!"

Again, silence, followed by the shifting of papers. "I'll tell you this. A guy by the name of Hawkins in the history department down there at Western Michigan University might be able to give you more."

"Is he the source on this?"

"Cal, I've already said too much. If you call him, you didn't get this from me."

"C'mon, Ben, I'm up to my ears on this."

"Talk to Hawkins."

I agreed. After we hung up, I stood by the window, trying to place the name. I thought of Melinda, who had mentioned a history class one time, something about it focusing on helping young people track down local historical sources.

I found the number for Hawkins and called. Amazingly, he answered on the first ring. But that was the best part of our short conversation. He clearly didn't want to talk to me.

"Just tell me this, sir," I said, trying to keep him on the line. "Did you have Melinda Blackwell as a student?"

"If I remember her correctly."

"And did you help her do research on local history or something like that?"

"Reverend, I have a class to teach. Let me think about this. Give me your number, so I can get back to you."

"But, this is important!"

"How did you get my name, Reverend?"

I wanted to tell him, hoping that might give me more credibility, but I didn't.

"Let me call you back," he said.

59

I went to the window again, watching the way the wind bent the stalks of corn and the gray clouds scudded across the sky.

I also thought about the casino.

Mine was a small congregation, and only a few were Native American. All along I had been ambiguous about a casino, which would be built about two miles to the south in Bradley. It was a fight that I hadn't fought, and a subject I tended to avoid.

Most of the Indians in my church opposed the casino. They saw it as bringing more problems than it would solve. But some favored it as well.

The fight to build a casino had been fought on many fronts, and I had tried all along to keep a low profile because I hated the thought of having to use gambling as the main source of income. Already there were far too many casinos in the state.

Yet, I also knew that the Native Americans of our area had few other options for making money. I ranged my memory, trying to recall anything Melinda might have said about her history class and if that somehow tied into the casino.

But it didn't take long for my mind to return to that day they had taken her body out of the lake. She had not drowned. Instead, someone had beaten and strangled her so hard that her neck had been broken. I had done the funeral, in a church in Kalamazoo. I still remembered the stricken look on her father's face. I had brought him from the hospital for the service. Promise me, Reverend, that you will help find my daughter's killer, he asked after the weeks dragged on and he grew sicker and the police came up with no leads.

Well, I thought, that is why I got involved with things like this. I should have said that to Monica last night.

I sat at my desk, ready to dial her number. But then I got another call, this one from Manny. What a day. He wanted to meet for lunch.

Sweat poured from my face as I hiked up Michigan Street Hill from my parking spot in the visitor's lot of The Grand Rapids Press. Yet another phone call that came into my study at church had convinced me that the sermon had to wait.

Since I had agreed to meet VanderMolen at 2 p.m., I decided to leave my truck at the paper, instead of trying to fight for a spot up the hill that had been transformed in the past three years into a mini-Mayo Clinic. Spectrum Hospital's huge campus, along with two research centers, massive parking structures and a glistening new health care services educational center for Grand Valley State University, took up four large city blocks.

Manny was drinking coffee at the Red Geranium, one of the few remaining independent, non-medical-related business on the Hill, when I arrived. He made a wisecrack about my lateness and asked me not to get my body fluids all over the table.

I told him I was sorry about making him wait.

"No problem, Pastor, you know that I've got all of the time in the world, especially when I'm in the middle of a homicide investigation."

"Have you cracked the case yet?"

"I thought that was why you wanted to buy me lunch?"

"I thought this was your idea?"

Manny smiled. "I forgot."

When the waitress stopped by, I asked for the special—roast pork, mashed potatoes, green beans and a corn muffin. The hungry man's meal.

Manny only wanted more coffee.

"You're not eating?" I asked.

"Not now."

Once the food arrived, Manny watched me chow down.

Finally, sopping gravy with the last of my muffin, I asked Rodriguez if he at least wanted dessert. "You go ahead," he said.

I ordered pecan pie and ice cream. The waitress, a pony-tailed woman with marginal teeth and a healthy body, wrote it down, re-filled Manny's mug, and went off to get my order. Her name was Darlene.

"You have a pretty healthy appetite for a minister who's just barely staying out of hot water," Manny said.

I leaned back. This diner was filled with folks from Spectrum Hospital, a table of beat cops, neighbors and a group of cable TV installers. This was where I went for lunch or breakfast a couple times a week when I'd served the church on South Division. One of my good friends referred to this place as Democratic Party Headquarters, since this was the only joint within blocks that didn't seem, my friend had said, overrun with slick-haired, expensive-suited young Republicans. This was still Jerry Ford country, after all. I didn't normally pig out like I was doing today.

"If I'm in so much trouble, how come I keep doing your job for you?" I asked Manny.

"How is that?"

"I hear that the guy's death may be tied in to the fight over the casino in my neck of the woods."

He cocked an eyebrow. I couldn't tell if this was a surprise. "Do tell."

"Does that line up with anything that you're hearing?"

"Pastor, I have to admit, you are charming." Without his bomber jacket, which hung on a hook by the door, Rodriguez looked less formidable. He wore a Detroit Lions sweatshirt, cut off at the sleeves, and a crisp white shirt under it. The man had always been a study in contrasts. He still looked tired, and probably had been on the go since the other night. I wondered how much to tell him.

"Does charming mean that I'm right?"

"Well, I hope you let me come along when you make an arrest," he said.

"Sarcasm is the weapon of the weak," I replied.

"Chaucer?"

"Who's that?"

I finished my pie and then worked on the ice cream. "So," he said, "how did your meeting go with the tattooed lady last night?"

And here I thought I was so smart.

I told him I had no idea what he was talking about.

He didn't even bother to call me a liar.

62

Darlene came and went, providing another refill. The lunch crowd was thinning. Manny looked out the window into the parking lot, where cars made their way along Michigan Street. "Did she know anything?" he finally asked. His gaze left the window and settled calmly on me.

I wondered how he knew where I'd been. But I didn't ask. Instead, I answered him straight up. "This is why you wanted to meet?"

"In part."

"Well, Dezi says she's checking it out."

He leaned closer to me. "And what did you and the chancellor talk about?"

I set my coffee cup on its plate. "You're following me."

"No, I talked to Monica. I tried to find you earlier and called her church when you weren't around."

"I was in my office all morning."

"Maybe your line was busy."

"She didn't return my call."

"I think she's mad at you."

"Did she tell you that?"

"I misspoke myself. Maybe the words are fed up."

I didn't like having him relay a message like that.

"And, so, what about the chancellor?"

"If you know so much about what I'm doing, why don't you …"

He held up a hand, as if to stop any more words. "Calvin, just tell what you know."

"And then you'll tell me about this map?"

"I don't know anything about that."

I decided to fill him in anyway. When I finished, he gazed in his coffee cup, as if searching for the next thing to say. Looking up, he asked, "Where did Lazio hear this bull about a map?"

"Is it bull, Manny?"

"Is it?"

I decided to tell him what Benny had told me. He listened very carefully and asked me to go over it again.

When I had, he slumped in his seat, thinking. He took out his beeper, checked it, put it away. He got another cup of coffee, sipped it, set it down. His mood had changed. I think what I had said had struck chords. "A map?" he asked.

I shrugged.

"Of what?"

I shrugged again. "Maybe tribal land."

Manny's eyes grew small. "Look, Calvin, I'm going to level with you."

"What a novel concept."

He didn't like that, but kept going. Essentially, the homicide detective let me know—amid a fair amount of grumbling and complaining about me sticking my nose into things—that he didn't mind if I was able to turn over a few stones to help this investigation.

That is, as long as I kept things legal and him informed. Letting a civilian like me into his confidence like this was a big deal, and doubtless ran counter to his cop's code of ethics. But it was clear Manny badly wanted to get to the bottom of the death. He wasn't happy about me upping the reward, seeing as how it had caused so much trouble already. Even so, he was obviously very anxious to come up with any good lead that might be out there. He let me know, of course, that the police chief would probably be livid when he learned about the new reward money.

He also had a warning.

"Your friend, Miss Dezi. I wouldn't trust her with a 10-foot pole. She no doubt can get information, because she been around the block a few times. But watch out for her, Cal. She's not above turning a trick when in need of cash. She's been known to drop a baggie of pot or two in the pockets of some of the slime who come in there to get tattooed."

"Can I trust her at all?"

Manny shrugged. "I also hear that maybe lately she found Jesus, so who knows, your guess is as good as mine."

"How about Wooly Bully?"

Manny thought about this. "He's a scumbag, plain and simple." Manny finished the dregs of his coffee and added: "But one more thing, Calvin."

I waited.

"If any of your Indian friends—or anyone else—down there say anything more about a map, you need to get with me right away."

"Do you think this is about a map—that someone would kill a young girl over a map?"

"Or Geronimo in the church?"

I nodded.

Manny put both hands on the top of the table, ready to hoist himself to his feet. "I'll say this, you have some pretty strong interests opposed to the casino, but murder, I don't know. I think there's a lot more to this than a map."

I loved my church out in the country with its open spaces, woods and streams. But I also still enjoyed the city.

From atop Michigan Street Hill you can see deep into the Grand River Valley—the low-lying swatch of land through which rolls the Grand River. Things cooked along out there today.

The water moved smoothly; wisps of smoke from factories floated through air; traffic slid in a steady stream along the freeways; downtown buildings caught flashes of the high-hanging sun; and the West Side neighborhoods shone in a comfortable, mid-afternoon splendor. Clouds were gone. A perfect early fall afternoon.

Spread before me was the city that in my youth was magical. We lived on a muck farm, southwest of here, not too far from the Lake Michigan shoreline. We made it into Grand Rapids every couple weeks or so and my early memories were of a bustling place with lots of old buildings and aging neighborhoods.

Urban renewal wiped out a fair chunk of the downtown I knew as a boy. In its place stood many new structures, a few towering over the city and etching into the sky a distinct outline. Some people liked to call our town Bland Rapids—and there had been good reason.

Not too many years ago, after they bulldozed many of the older neighborhoods to make way for progress, if you could call it that, they erected a bunch of exquisitely dour structures to house city, county and some banking services. Only in the last dozen years had character begun to show its face in some new, more interesting structures, including a new convention center whose swooping shape appeared on the left as I walked down the hill.

Michigan's second-largest city was starting to take on a vitality that was evident in the handful of building projects under way, and others that has been recently completed. It was almost like our once sedate Dutch Reformed enclave was building its muscles and broadening its shoulders, starting to gear up to take on a more prominent place in the wider world.

As I walked, I considered Manny's words about Dezi and cautioned myself not to leap too quickly at anything she offered. I knew I should be back in my office. I needed to dig through the rest of the mail and get back to my Sunday sermon.

But I put off the office and started up the steps to The Grand Rapids Press. Once inside, I took the escalator to the second-floor editorial office. On the way, I paused a moment to examine the huge, wall-size mural showing scenes from the front pages of the city's only newspaper. World events were captured there in slashes of color. Images of front pages mixed with those of reporters hustling off to cover stories.

Once I stepped into the editorial reception area, I asked the white-haired woman behind the desk if I could see Randy VanderMolen, the religion editor.

She called an extension, told someone I was here and then buzzed me through the locked doors and into the newsroom.

Brightly lit and cavernous, the area in which the writers and editors did their thing was relatively quiet this afternoon. I'd been in here many times, often on church business or for other stories.

The reporter with whom I was most familiar was VanderMolen, who now hailed me in the hallway separating the press library from the bank of desks at which many of the reporters sat.

A chubby, disheveled character who took his job very seriously, VanderMolen gave me a smile and asked if I was going to the press conference Monica scheduled for 3 p.m. at Bicentennial Park, the open, grassy area in front of the Ford Presidential Museum.

This stopped me dead in my tracks. "What press conference?" I asked.

"I can't believe that she's getting the Dalai Lama to come to River City," he said.

His words hit me like a punch. Monica hadn't said anything about this. "You mean, the one from Tibet?"

"Is there another?"

I tried to keep cool. Though I was in the dark, I covered my tracks as best I could. "Quite the deal, yes?" I asked VanderMolen.

The religion writer looked a little dubious, as if he had caught how off balance I was. "No doubt."

"This is what you wanted to talk to me about?" I asked.

"It's big news."

VanderMolen led me into the newsroom and had me sit in a chair by his surprisingly neat desk. Before I answered his questions, I reminded him that I'd come with a purpose of my own.

Joe Casey, the cop reporter, meanwhile waltzed up. He had a bottle of Mountain Dew in his hand. I knew him as an Irishman who had often prowled for stories on the streets outside my storefront church on Division. He and I exchanged sarcastic pleasantries, and then he slugged back the pop and leaned close. Around us spread a sea of desks, at which men and women were either talking on phones or writing stories. I felt the soft hum of news being churned in the air.

"So what's the latest skinny on the murder in the cathedral?" Casey asked.

"Not much." I swiveled around in the seat, facing him better.

"Are you stonewalling me, Reverend?"

"Would I do that to you?"

"Is the pope Catholic? Wait, I'm sorry. Wrong religion. Was John Calvin a malcontent?"

We went on like that for a while, and then I offered my morsel of news. "I have more money for the reward, which now includes the man in church."

Casey's reporter's pad seemed to appear out of thin air.

"How much?"

"Thirty grand."

His eyebrows went up. "Who's the benefactor?"

I pretended to lock my lips with a key.

"C'mon, you can't do that to me."

"Sorry."

Casey looked at Randy. "Who's going to write this?"

"Be my guest," said the religion editor.

Fifteen or so minutes later, both he and VanderMolen had what they wanted from me—a comment or two about Monica and most of what I knew about the cathedral murder. I left out the part about the murder weapon, since Manny yesterday asked me to keep my mouth shut on that.

But before wrapping it up, I asked Casey if he knew of any gang that had tattoos of Geronimo on them.

He perked up, knowing this linked to the cathedral murder. "Describe it better."

I did.

Casey rubbed his chin when I had finished. "That one is new to me." He had done a big newspaper series a year or two before on local gangs. "But I have a couple sources I could check."

I told him that I appreciated it.

"The dead guy have this tattoo on him?" Casey then asked.

He scowled and swore when I once again pretended to lock my lips.

"One more thing?" I asked.

Casey smiled. "We're doing you all the favors?"

"I'm wondering. In covering the proposed casino in Wayland, has anyone ever mentioned some kind of hidden map?"

68

Both Casey and VanderMolen laughed. "A hidden treasure or something?" asked the cop reporter, smiling.

Again, I filled them in, aware of how much help they could be. And help, all the help I could get, was what I needed.

"A map strikes me as ridiculous. But I'll talk to our business desk," said Casey. "See what they can tell us."

CHAPTER ELEVEN

Traffic zoomed by on I-196, maybe 100 yards behind me. A handful of dignitaries—a city commissioner, a church leader or two, and the Reverend Monica Smit—milled about on the small stage erected just this side of the smoothly flowing Grand River. Monica had whipped this thing together in record time. But she was always like that—organization was her strength. I think mine is creating and then dealing with chaos.

The white-façaded, wedge-shaped Ford Museum, in front of which spewed a fancy fountain, stood to my right. Contained inside the former president's museum was a bunch of memorabilia from Ford's career, starting as a school boy in town, moving on to his football-playing days at the University of Michigan and then encompassing his time in politics. A striking replica of the Oval Office, replete with a thick rug bearing the presidential seal, was displayed on the second floor. A photo of him stumbling off Air Force One hung in there someplace.

But my mind didn't dally long on the fake room in the White House as I walked with VanderMolen along the cement path into the hilly park. Bathed in sunlight, some of it reflected off the river, Monica looked striking. She paced the stage with grace, her golden hair gently touched by the clean breeze. Her success had sculpted her, made her more confident, and shaped her in ways that made her seem increasingly foreign and yet a little exotic to me.

Up ahead I saw a gaggle of reporters setting up to take down or tape the news conference.

"Randy, is the Dalai Lama really that big of a news story?"

He gave me a funny look. "It's not every day our town gets showered by the likes of the world's most famous Buddhist."

On the way here he told me that the Dalai Lama had agreed to speak at the ecumenical gathering of church leaders, including Monica, set to take place in the new convention center in early November. I still felt ticked off. Monica had mentioned the ecumenical meeting—of a large committee of the World Council of Churches—but she hadn't said a thing about the Dalai Lama.

"How could she get him on such short notice, do you think?" asked VanderMolen.

I thought about it and hit on an idea. "Well, he does have a center down near Indianapolis, and also I think his biographer teaches at U-M. He's got ties to the Midwest."

"But it's great, the Buddhist of all Buddhists showing up in Christian Reformed territory," the reporter said.

"Right."

I left VanderMolen with his chums from the Fourth Estate and stepped under the overhang of a tree, gazing beyond the stage at the smoothly shaped Indian mounds that flanked the entry to a pedestrian bridge over the Grand. This park went by two names, one tying back to the country's Bicentennial, the year Ford was president, and the same year I left the Navy and landed in Seattle, where I took a job as a paramedic-in-training.

The other name of this gently rolling park was Ah-Nab-Awen, an Annishabe name meaning meeting place. All along the Grand, Indians had met for centuries, trading and holding ceremonies after the hunting season. Members of my church had relatives who had participated. Just south of here was an area where real Indian burial mounds, not the ones represented in this park, stood.

I heard the sharp screech of static and someone tapping a microphone. It was one of the city commissioners, a short, silver-haired woman by the name of Betty Williamson, a local patron of the arts and strong supporter of ecumenical activities, as well as a big backer of Monica.

Betty welcomed everyone and thanked us for coming on such short notice. She then said that the city had an important announcement linked to next month's meeting here of the Ecumenical Forum.

"I think we all know how bringing the World Council here has been an important feather in our cap for our new convention center. But here to tell you about an important addition to the program is Reverend Monica Smit, who met our main speaker just recently at a large meeting overseas. Before she left for overseas, I asked jokingly to see if she could get an important person to attend. Little did any of us know what that would mean to our city. Here is Reverend Monica Smit to tell you about it."

Warm sun beat down on us. The river rolled and the skyline of our medium-size Midwest city shimmered across the way as my long-time girlfriend took the mike and started in. The new convention center stretched almost directly across from me.

Monica didn't milk the situation. She cut to the quick, telling the crowd about how she had a chance to meet and recently spend unexpected time with the man the world knows as the Dalai Lama. She explained how she learned that he would be traveling in the United States in November—to attend a gathering at a huge Tibetan center in Indiana and then to make a stop to pick up an honorary doctorate at the University of Notre Dame. Almost on a lark, she asked if he might be willing to speak at the forum. Amazingly, he said he would look at his schedule. Last night, when she got home, she said, she found an e-mail from his office informing her that he could attend.

"We're so very grateful for this," she said, her voice ringing across the open park. "By his coming, and with leaders from many different faith groups, the forum meeting here in Grand Rapids will probably prove to be significant in a way we hadn't even imagined."

Monica scanned the small crowd, glancing vaguely at me. "God's grace is certainly active here."

The press conference didn't last long, and within minutes the stage was next to empty. I leaned against the tree, battling a mixture of feelings.

"Hey, stranger."

Monica was walking my way, a mild expression of concern on her scrubbed pinkish face.

"The Dalai Lama," I said. "That's great."

"Isn't it?"

We stared at each other, unspoken words colliding between us.

A couple people came up, wanting to talk to Monica, asking what the Dalai Lama is really like.

Knowing I'd best not leave, I waited until she was done, and then we strolled along the path beyond the stage to the bridge by the Indian mounds.

We didn't talk as we started across the structure, heading in the direction of where the historic Welsh Auditorium once stood. The spot now contained part of the convention center.

About halfway across the bridge, we stopped and leaned over the rail, watching the water roll west toward Lake Michigan. Many years ago, when the Indians set up shop here, the spot in the river frothed with rapids. No longer. They had been flattened to make smooth water for sport fishermen and the occasional boater. The shore, once meeting grounds for trade, had become an urbanized setting for trade of another kind altogether.

"So, what's bugging you, Calvin?"

"Our town," I said, waving a hand at the skyline beyond us, "just ain't what it used to be."

"You're being nostalgic?"

I felt heavy and thick, dragged down by what I knew was petty jealousy. I turned to her, "I'm not feeling nostalgic."

"What then?"

It was such a nice late summer afternoon. A few people passed us on the bridge. Motors from big machines growled in the distance, muffled by the greater noise of traffic, flowing water and the voices of people out enjoying the weather.

But the weather was much trickier from where I was standing. "Why didn't you tell me anything about the Dalai Lama?"

"I didn't know for sure until I checked my e-mail at home last night."

"But there was a good chance?"

She shrugged.

"Was it a state secret?"

"You were so busy with whatever it is you're doing that I didn't think it was time to mention it."

"Come on. Give me a break."

"No, you give me a break, Calvin. You're so busy playing cops and robbers, handing out rewards."

"And getting knocked for a loop by a killer in the cathedral."

Monica's face fell. That was a low blow, I knew.

Then I saw tears in her eyes. "Calvin, what's wrong with you?" Her voice trembled. I didn't reply to her question, unsure how to answer, a little taken aback by the emotion.

"Why can't we get along? What is it? Are you jealous?" Her words tugged at me, but there was a gulf between us I couldn't ignore.

"Look, Monica, the least you could have done is mention it. VanderMolen asked me about it. Heck, he knew before me."

"Sorry."

Our ministries, our personalities, even events were yanking us in different directions. I waited a few moments before my better judgment kicked in. "My suggestion is we call a truce," I said.

"Calvin, I'm not at war with you. I just wish you weren't so darned bullheaded and paid attention to people other than yourself and your duty or whatever it is you think you have to do in this thing."

"Thing!"

"I feel bad, too, about that man who died on Sunday. And you know how I feel about what happened to that young woman from your church. But, Calvin, it's not my job to solve those things. It's not my job to ignore everything else to try to do something that isn't yours to do."

"It isn't, then whose job is it?"

"Manny, for one."

Three businessmen walked by. I thought of my promise, and it suddenly seemed so useless, so silly, a matter of ego, to try to find

74

out what happened to Melinda Blackwell. But then, her father had pleaded. I thought of the serene expression on her face on the day of her baptism, and then of the body from the lake.

We started walking, heading back into the park. We didn't speak as we headed toward her car. Our hands brushed and I felt my heart ache.

"Monica," I finally said. "We can't go on like this."

"How?"

"See-sawing, back and forth, making no commitment."

"I know."

"I think we need help," I said.

"Such as?"

"From a wise person who can tell us where we went wrong and where to go from here."

"Like who?" Monica asked.

"Well, does your friend from Tibet do couple's counseling?"

She stopped, eyeing me with wariness. But then I smiled, and we both cracked up and ended up in a hug that felt so good that it hurt.

I took a walk through downtown, sorting through several things, including my inscrutable relationship with Monica, before heading over to pick up my car at The Press. I then decided to stop in at St. Mary's Hospital to see a former church member who was in there for back surgery, and followed that by eating a quick, solitary dinner at the Elite Diner near my old church. My cell rang just as I left the restaurant. Dezi told me she wanted to meet. Even though she refused to even hint at what she wanted, I told her to meet me at the restaurant. She said she wouldn't be there for an hour or so. I suggested we meet in Wayland. She didn't like that, and so I suggested meeting outside my old storefront church, just across from the Elite.

Not long after, I shuffled across South Division to the church. Pham, the janitor, answered my knock on the door. He was a small, wrinkled, leather-tough man who had spent years in a prison camp outside Hanoi before coming here. We'd gotten pretty close before I left to take the other church. We chewed the fat for a few minutes and then, as he hustled off to get the conference room ready for a meeting of some sort, I slipped into the dark sanctuary for a few minutes alone.

With the lights off and shades drawn, I took time for prayer, to ask God for direction. Was I indeed on an ego trip? I wondered, thinking both of my reluctance to commit to Monica as well as my attempt to find Melinda's—and now the Geronimo guy's—killer, assuming the same person murdered them both.

Preachers can easily get carried away with their self-importance. Even the best of us can start thinking we have a unique line to the divine and that our promises, our ideas, our beliefs are somehow ordained. But I didn't feel that way tonight.

I was still there, still full of questions, on my knees at 8 p.m. as people started to show up for the meeting at the church.

Pham had coffee brewing and snacks ready in the conference room, set just off the main sanctuary that showed out onto Division Avenue. It brought back memories.

I liked my mission parish, not part of my former denomination, but missed this place. It was in an old building that contained a maze of rooms. The worship space was open and relatively unadorned. But it had had its tensions and trials. I had left two years before, to do some graduate work in Kalamazoo, and then to take the church in the country. No longer a CRC pastor, I felt freer, less bound by what I considered silly rules.

I greeted and spoke to members of the board, four local business-men, a college professor, a couple former street people who credited Heartside with helping turn their lives around, and three women who lived in the suburbs but dedicated themselves to the inner city.

Then, I saw Dezi shoving her face against the glass, cupping her eyes with her hands. I opened the door and stepped outside.

Cars whizzed by in the dark.

"Can we talk?" she asked. She wore a bulky buckskin coat.

"You want to come inside?"

"Can we go for a walk or something?"

We headed south along Division, in the direction of the cathedral.

Although a chill clung to the air, she took off her coat, revealing a very tight and sheer-looking blouse. Sex as a weapon, I thought, or at the very least a negotiating tool.

By the time we'd made it halfway to the cathedral, I decided to sweeten the pot and told her I could offer more money for help in getting the name. I smelled her perfume, a strong fruity odor and noticed the thick powder on her face. Tattoos wove like dusky lace on her shoulders. Her breasts, well, I'm human. I'll leave it at that.

"How much money are we talking?" she asked.

I couldn't tell if it was greed I saw on her face or fear or even the anxious expression of a person trying to pull a fast one. "It's yours if we get names and it leads us to the killer – or killers."

"How much?"

"Fifty-five thousand dollars."

She whistled.

We crossed the street between a parking lot and the block on which the cathedral stood. Its sharp spires cut into the sky, the stained-glass windows were dark as death—an image that made me shudder.

"Then are you up for driving down to Detroit?" Dezi asked.

I stopped. "What?"

She explained, "We'll need to talk to someone there."

"They don't have a phone?"

We went around on this for a minute or two, but she was adamant. "Look, take it or leave it," she said.

"When do you want to go?"

"It probably should be tomorrow."

By this time we were near the back door of the cathedral, the one Bob and I had exited after I got bushwhacked. We stopped. I thought of Dezi and Bob dancing.

"I'm supposed to take Bob to the dentist tomorrow morning," I told her.

"Bring the big guy along."

CHAPTER TWELVE

We headed southeast on I-96 toward Motown in my Ranger. Dezi sat next to the door, with Bob sandwiched between us. I had picked her up about 10 a.m. outside her apartment. Clad in her buckskin coat and sporting tiny red ribbons in her newly dyed blonde hair, she had looked groggy then and still did now.

Monica's brother stayed on his best behavior; his hair slicked back, hands resting on his lunch box, a silly smile on his face. If the drill at the dentist's office had bothered him, you wouldn't know it now. He kept stealing glances at Dezi who, as far as I could tell, ignored him. She finally stirred long enough to ask me to stop at the next rest top. Her face looked puffy, the lipstick shiny on her wide mouth.

I slowed as we reached the exit for Ionia, a town about 30 miles east of Grand Rapids. Sliding into the right lane, I aimed for the ramp.

Less than a minute later, I wheeled into a Total station just off the interstate and parked. Dezi checked for something in her purse and then, without saying anything, shouldered open the door. Bob had a puppy-dog look on his face, big jaw dropping as she hustled for the restroom. I patted his shoulder.

"Let's get some coffee," I said.

We had returned by the time Dezi finally emerged from the can, stepping quickly toward us. She had make-up on her eyes and cheeks and had taken most of the ribbons out of her new hairdo. Once in, she shook off the buckskin and stuffed it by the huge purse at her feet.

"You get me coffee, too?" she wondered, a liquid brightness in her eyes.

I did and handed it over. Bob offered a donut, which she took gladly and munched as I guided us back to the freeway. When he gave her another donut, she leaned over and kissed his cheek.

"Thanks, Big Guy."

Bob dipped his head, his cheeks coloring. He wore his Green Bay Packers get-up, the same one from two nights before, although it had been laundered.

As I drove, I tried not to think of all the work left for me at the church. I hoped we'd be back by dinner. Two and a half hours down, maybe an hour there, if that, and back.

Adding to things: I had only gotten a couple hours of sleep. After taking the walk with Dezi last night, I decided to go running. Often a few hard miles around midnight puts me in the mood for sleep.

I took a route that led me south and east along dark country roads, out of Wayland and back. In the home stretch, as I trotted down Main Street, I had a little conversation with God, questioning whether I should make this trip to Detroit. Images of my caller, under the blanket on the gurney and then on the slab in the morgue, drifted in and out as I had the conversation. In the end, the reasons for going outweighed the reasons for staying.

Dezi told me we were going to a neighborhood that bordered highly industrial downriver Detroit by the Ambassador Bridge that led into Canada.

I'd been down there before, twice in recent years for an annual ecumenical forum that brought together Christians, Muslims and Jews, at a large community center in an area called Del Ray. Given all of the unrest in the world, much of it spawned by religion, these gatherings, instituted after the devastating events of September 11, 2001, were one way of trying to bring about peace and understanding.

Dezi had said after I picked her up that we were supposed to talk to the grandmother—or maybe she was the aunt—of the man who died in the cathedral.

Near the I-496 cutoff to Lansing, a flurry of roadwork slowed us down. Guys in hard hats and orange vests labored among hulking machines. As I put on my brakes, a big white pick-up truck appeared in my rear-view mirror. It nearly hit me, but veered into the left lane and shot past. A pair of Tasmanian Devils waved at me from the mud flaps. The driver, a guy with a white beard, gave me a quick look before glancing away.

I had to wait for a few minutes for my heart to stop pounding.

Once we'd cleared the roadwork, Dezi craned around Bob. She seemed nervous again. I eyed that purse, and she saw me do it, but ignored the implied criticism. "Mind if I smoke?"

I did, but told her to go ahead. Cracking her window, she leaned back in the seat. Smoke swirled around us like a veil. I waved some away with my hand and rolled my window down all of the way.

Dezi watched me make a fuss with an edge of petulance. Then she changed gears.

"How'd you talk me into this?" she asked. Bob was pretending to play the banjo.

"I think money had something to do with it," I replied.

Dezi kept smoking, tendrils wafting out the window. "That's right."

Bob stopped playing the imaginary instrument, popped open his lunch box and offered her a sandwich. Dezi waved him off.

I waited her out, sensing she had something to say. Just as we hit the outskirts of Brighton, she came out with it.

"The thing is, Reverend, the people we might be dealing with here are… pretty nasty." She spoke in a dull voice. "I mean, I've dealt with them before."

"I thought we were talking to the grandmother or an aunt or whatever?"

"I had to go through a few people to get her name."

I asked her what people.

"Former friends. One who owed me a big favor."

"And this is it?"

"You could say that."

We rode awhile in silence, my fingers tapping the wheel. I thought about what Manny had said about Dezi. I wondered what she was getting us into. "How nasty are these people?" I asked.

She didn't answer for a minute or so, then leaned over and looked at me. "You probably ought to know, I've got a gun in my purse."

CHAPTER THIRTEEN

After mentioning the firepower she packed, Dezi reached into her huge leather purse. But instead of dragging out a gun to show me, she came up with the most important weapon of all—a Bible.

"Are you into prophesy, Reverend?"

"Depends on the forecast. How about you?"

"I grew up Seventh-Day Adventist."

I found her full of surprises. Even so, I didn't want to talk religion. I wanted to know more about what and whom we faced once we reached Detroit. But she started reading the Book of Revelation aloud to Bob.

He, of course, loved all of the fiery descriptions of how the world was going to end. I'd be inclined to say the complex theology was way over his head, but you never know.

I found it discomforting to have Dezi reading about the rapturous, Earth-rending ways of the Lord to Monica's brother.

But at some point I stopped paying attention, tucked away my questions, and just drove.

By 1 p.m. we started rolling through the industrial-park-pocked outskirts of Detroit. I took the I-296 cutoff near Farmington and zipped along the far, western edge of the Motor City, driving through a handful of suburbs, entering the city limits and then went by Ford's massive Rouge Plant. I had two uncles on my mother's side who spent their careers inside that grimy place. Soon, on the left we passed a huge white monstrosity that turned out to be the MGM Grand, one of Detroit's casinos under construction.

"Which way again?" I asked as I approached the exit to the Ambassador Bridge.

Dezi set aside her Bible, which she had been reading silently, and dug a folded paper from her coat. "We just passed the exit."

I gave her a dirty look, and she returned it with a defiant stare.

So I got off at the Ambassador Bridge, which ran over to Canada, and pulled up at the light for Fort Street. Cars and trucks filled the entryway to the bridge, all likely to undergo close scrutiny in these days of international temper tantrums.

"Go left here," Dezi said, running a finger over the writing. "Wait, no that's OK. Actually we only have to go back a mile or two."

She looked a little guilty when I threw her another irritated glance. "Are you sure?"

"Get off my case, Reverend. I made a mistake, OK?"

She showed me the hand-drawn map, pointing her finger to an area near Livernois and Michigan Avenue. It wasn't too far.

"More," Bob said, meaning from the Good Book.

"Later."

I made a turn. The abandoned, former headquarters of the Michigan Central Railroad rose about a half-mile to the east. It was sad to see it in such sorry shape. Twice I'd ridden out of there, once with my mom to see friends in Chicago, and another time on a Future Farmers of America jaunt to Washington, D.C. Not far from that loomed the red brick spires of St. Anne's, the oldest Catholic church in Michigan.

The sidewalks were mostly empty as we drove down Fort Street. Large factories, several boarded up, lined the road. Downtown Detroit spread in the distance, its buildings standing tall amid a fair amount of devastation and some urban reconstruction. On our left ran an ugly pink wall, separating the neighborhood from the freeway and bridge traffic.

A weedy lot or two opened as we entered Mexican Town. A burly dark-haired man was spraying water on a colorful mural of dancers painted on the side of a restaurant. A few other businesses also had artwork scrolled on the walls.

I had to stop a moment to ask a pedestrian for directions before being able to loop through Mexican Town and get on Vernor Highway, a busy four-lane lined by tire stores, small restaurants, storefront churches, a Detroit Police substation and other businesses.

Finally, Livernois appeared up ahead. Sad-looking businesses, many boarded up, gutted homes, sick-looking trees and a party store or two with metal bars over the windows showed us more of the city.

I took Livernois north, struck by the Third World poverty of the run-down homes and businesses. We crossed under a large railroad trestle and rode alongside a small city park filled with what looked to be homeless men lounging lazily on benches and the ground.

"My dad used to live in this lousy area," said Dezi.

"Did he work around here?" I asked.

"If you can call it that."

"What about your mom?"

"She died when I was born." Dezi peered out the window and checked her map. "Michigan's coming up. Go left."

Soon, we rode by another strip of devastation—a sprawling warehouse with broken windows, dirty bricks and an empty parking lot. But then we slipped into Dearborn and suddenly the urban landscape changed. Once again we passed healthy businesses. I had an idea what they did and sold, but wasn't sure, because much of the writing was in Arabic—that delicate swirled script that made no sense to me at all.

"Here, Western Avenue, make a left."

Moments later we pulled in front of a three-story aluminum-sided home. Its roof needed replacing, but a few flowers and shrubs were neatly planted in the front. It looked to be in better shape than several of the nearby homes. Just across the street was the burned-out shell of a house. Weeds and scrubby trees surrounded that place. I wasn't sure whether we were still in Dearborn or in Detroit again.

Outside, we gathered on the sidewalk. A mildly dilapidated wooden porch wrapped around the front of the house and disappeared along the left side. I watched Dezi search inside that magic purse for something, the harsh sun showing small red marks in her face, as well the dark roots of her hair, places she had missed with the dye. She had slipped the buckskin coat around her shoulders, even though it was mild, the temperature in the 60s. Bob was pretending to shoot Blue Jays fighting in a nearby tree.

I made for the porch. They followed.

Under a list of names taped to numbered mailboxes by the front door was a buzzer. Dezi leaned in and thumbed apartment three. When there was no answer, Dezi buzzed again, and then stepped back, hugging her shoulders. Her eyes had lost their luster; her skin was thick with make up. Bob rocked on his heels, looking anxious.

"Who told you about this woman, Dezi?"

"Like I said, a friend. We used to work together at Four Seasons."

"What's that?"

"A dance club not too far from here."

"Modern dance?"

"Ha-ha."

Bob turned to me, cupping his groin, showing me he had to pee. I told him to wait.

No response from the buzzer, even after I gave the button a push.

"Just go in," said Dezi.

I wasn't so sure about that, but she stepped forward, opened the screen and tried the front door. It opened and we stepped into a dim, spacious hallway. A couple bikes, a rolled up hose and a pile of newspapers sat in a corner. A staircase led up on the right. After checking numbers on the doors, I went that way.

"Hey, Rev, the big guy has to tap a kidney."

I paused, peering down. A small, beveled glass window cast oblong shapes on them. Bob still grabbed himself, giving me plaintive eyes. "Hang on, Sport. This shouldn't take long." I jerked my head at Dezi. "Aren't you coming?"

But she didn't move.

"Does this woman have a name?"

"Mary Simon."

84

"And she is?"

"She might be the grandma of the dead guy."

"Might or is?"

"Might." Tired of her, I went it alone.

At the top of the stairs, I ran into a small, carpeted hallway. I heard the front door close. When nature called, Bob had to answer, sometimes without benefit of facilities. Dezi probably had her own needs to consider—these different than reading the Bible.

I found number three down the hall on the right. I stepped over and knocked. The hallway smelled of foreign food, spices not familiar to my nostrils. But they sure woke up my stomach. I'd missed lunch. I should have grabbed one of the baloney sandwiches Bob had brought along in his lunchbox.

I knocked again.

As a minister I'd had to bear bad tidings many times, but never found it easy. Sure, I'd driven here to find a name and maybe some background on the man in the cathedral. But I now feared I might have to inform a grandmother about the suspicious death. No telling how she'd take it. It also struck me that we still weren't absolutely sure that the dead guy had been my caller. He might have been the killer. Which still left us with trying to ID Geronimo.

Two more knocks drew nothing, so I stuck my ear to the door, trying to catch any sign of life inside. I strained, picking up what sounded like the refrigerator.

"Can I help you?"

Startled, I spun, almost lost my balance, and confronted a woman. She was all bones and sharp angles, her skin tight and ruddy. Purple veins skewered her cheeks. She held a Mason jar filled with plum-colored liquid in one hand. I hadn't noticed a light bulb going on, but it glowed from the ceiling behind her. The woman looked to be in her forties. She sipped from the jar, watching me.

"I'm looking for Mary Simon."

"Who are you?"

I gave her my name and my job title as she sipped carefully from the brew. She wore baggy jeans and an orange Denver Bronco jersey. Her straw-colored hair was covered by a bandana. "Why do you want to talk to her?" She gestured at the door with her jar.

"It's personal."

"So's trespassing."

"You live here?"

"I'm the landlady."

The downstairs door opened and the dynamic duo returned. They stomped their feet, as if shaking off snow. "Cool it! You'll wake my husband," yelled the landlady.

"So," she said, returning to me, "should I call the police?"

I decided to give a quick, edited rundown of why I was here.

Dezi, meanwhile, made her way up the stairs, coming to a stop on the landing a few steps down. She looked pudgy and pale, stuffed into her tight clothes, the coat looped over an arm. A dull gleam shone in her eyes. She'd hitched her mini skirt higher. "She's not there?" asked Dezi.

The landlady slugged some of the purple liquid, making a face, as if this one scorched her throat. I waited for her to answer Dezi's question, fearing she was going to shut us out.

"What kind of a preacher are you?" she asked.

"I'm trustworthy, loyal, friendly, brave, clean and confident."

"You preach for the Boy Scouts?"

"Actually, I'm Christian Reformed but now serving a community church."

She sipped her brew, thinking it over. "My dead uncle was Christian Reformed, up in Grand Rapids. He married into it."

"I'm sorry to hear that."

This got a laugh. "Look," she said, "the old lady got real sick on Sunday and they had to take her to the hospital."

"What was wrong with her?"

"She got beat up."

This set me back. "By who?"

"I'm not sure, since I wasn't home." She finished off her booze, and then looked straight at me.

"Were the police called?"

The landlady eyed me carefully.

I stepped into the rank, force field of her plum liquor. "Who beat her up, ma'am?"

"Talk to the priest over at St. Lazar's. He was the one who came and then called for the ambulance."

It took more coaxing, but she told me the location of the church— not far from her apartment house. That's all I got out of her.

St. Lazar's was a small brick-sided church on a side street off Michigan, down the block from a mosque in front of which a few men and women stood. I assumed they had just finished with their afternoon prayer. In many ways, I admired the Islamic faith, with its focus on intense, daily prayer and submission to the will of God. For them the divine was a real, everyday presence—and not something worshipped only on Sundays.

Unlike the Muslim place of worship, activity at the Catholic church was next to non-existent.

Wedged into a working-class neighborhood, St. Lazar's looked well-tended, the lawn mowed, flowers blooming along the walk leading to what looked to be a church office attached to one side of the church.

I got out and made for the door, where I rang the bell and was quickly met by an older man with a drooping black mustache who told me that Father Frank Zerba was either at the neighborhood out- reach center or had gone home for a late lunch. The man looked Middle Eastern, his dark eyes gazing at me with an ancient kind of sadness. I got directions for the outreach center and went back to the truck, where Dezi and Bob were pillaging his lunch box.

Other parts of Dearborn were fairly upscale, if I remembered correctly, and the Ford Motor Company headquarters—the Glass House, they called it—was located only a couple miles from where we were. But this part of the city bordering Detroit was older, the buildings reflecting a weary, factory-town kind of flavor. Empty lots choked with weeds and a gas station featuring rusty wire around a small yard piled with tires and oily engines caught my attention as I drove.

I soon found St. Lazar's Neighborhood Center, just this side of Detroit, stuck in a row of businesses that sold car parts, cheap furniture, ice cream, bicycles and, of all things, accessories for pleasure boats.

Once again I left Bob and Dezi. The lady behind the desk inside the center informed me that Father Zerba had just left for lunch. She sat on a chair with rollers and was moving back and forth between file cabinets. A few young women lined a nearby wall, many holding or tending to children. I took it that they were waiting for an afternoon health clinic.

"Where's he eating lunch?" I asked as the woman stuffed a thick folder into a metal drawer.

She gave me a very serious once over, as if wondering if my intentions for the priest were above board and decent. Apparently assuming I was as innocent as I no doubt pretended to look, she answered: "St. Anne's, down by the bridge. That's where he lives."

The bells of the big Catholic church boomed out the noon hour as I stepped up the walk to the rectory. Next to me rose the massive Romanesque house of worship, its red bricks sandblasted bright and clean, stained-glass windows lining one whole side of the building. We'd seen it on the way in. Up close it was even more impressive.

When a secretary wearing a Habitat for Humanity T-shirt answered the door, I said over the still-clanging clamor of the bells that I wanted to talk to Father Zerba, if he was still here.

"Well, you can try to catch him," she said, pointing at the steps of the church, where I saw a tall man loping along. "The janitor's sick, so he's got to fix the bells." She smiled and put her hands to her ears.

I took off after him. Bob and Dezi watched impassively from inside the truck, which I'd parked at the curb.

I jogged up the stone stairs and into the vestibule of the church.

The sound of the bells was slightly muffled in here. On the left ran a hallway lined with candles, a rack of pamphlets and a coat tree. The sanctuary was straight ahead; I noticed the crucifix at the front. I loved the inside of churches, except for when they contained dead bodies. On the right, I heard clacking heels. "Father Zerba!" I called.

"Yes?" Following the sound of his voice, I spotted him on my right, paused at the end of another hallway by a staircase.

I trotted that way, knowing I was imposing, but not caring. I came to a stop a couple feet from a tall, rugged-looking man with a shiny forehead and tufts of dark gray hair. He wore a hooded sweatshirt, faded jeans and grimy high-top tennis shoes. A man of God who didn't dress the part. I liked him already, even though he pinched his thin lips together and glowered at me.

As I quickly explained who I was and why I was here, his craggy face softened. He had stuffed his hands inside the wide sleeves of his sweatshirt.

We stood in a dim hallway, surrounded by shadows and small, framed pictures of what looked to be this church in various stages of construction. Set along the river, I knew this was the area in which the French first worshipped. This church, with its illustrious history, seemed to stand as a silent sentinel around us, making me think of the slow passage of time, as the priest pondered what I'd told him. Finally, he said: "Let's talk up there." He pointed up the stairway.

A couple minutes later I stood on a rail-enclosed ledge, maybe a dozen feet below the bell tower, while the priest reprogrammed the device that caused the bells to ring.

Up here the sound was even worse.

Trying to ignore the infernal noise, I looked out on the Ambassador Bridge and the hazy sprawl of Windsor. The husk of that massive railroad building stood on my right, and just below two of my favorite people played in a small park: Bob and Dezi. She was pushing him on a swing. Monica's brother had his arms looped around the chain and hands covering his ears.

Finally, the sound of the church bells ceased. I felt myself relax. Bob was still cupping his ears. Only when Dezi came around and eased his hands away did he let go.

"What's your denomination again?" The priest had joined me at the rail.

"Christian Reformed. We're a little smaller than the Catholics."

"That's the one that's in Grand Rapids."

"You've got it."

"Calvin College, right?"

I decided not to get into the community church thing. "Yup. We own it."

Father Zerba had a worn, intelligent face, a little tattered around the edges. He then told me, as I tried to get things straight as to where he worked, that he was a Glenmary Mission Father, living at St. Anne's, but serving as pastor of St. Lazar's, which apparently had been on the skids of late. Hence, he had been called here from overseas, Italy actually, to try to turn things around.

"You had a church over there?"

"I was teaching theology at a college in Rome. Do you serve a parish church?"

I told him about the small country church, mentioning that I had a few Native Americans as members.

He brightened. "I'm a small part Navajo, but mostly Greek."

"An odd combination. I'm nearly all Dutch, although my mom was Catholic."

As we spoke, a down-bound ore boat, as long as three football fields, sliced a rippling traffic pattern on the river north of the bridge. The two cities in two different countries busied themselves around us, chugging into midday, under a soot-smeared sky. Finally, I asked him about Mary Simon.

He frowned at my question.

"I heard someone beat her up."

The priest got a troubled look on his face. "I think it was her nephew."

90

I was all ears, and then some. "Do you know the nephew?"

"Only by reputation."

Now Bob and Dezi sat under a tree, reading the leather-bound Bible and eating out of his lunchbox. I wondered just how much food he had in that thing.

"Do you know his name, Father?" I asked.

The priest turned to me, those arms stuck up his sleeves again. I pegged him to be about fifty, a few years older than me. His face reminded me of a well-oiled catcher's mitt. Sprigs of gray hair sprouted from his nose. "Sorry, I don't know."

Streets crisscrossed below. On the left stretched a row of buildings, moving off toward downtown. The sky was clear blue, the day smelled of autumn. Sun played on that abandoned railroad building, highlighting the gutted places.

"Does Mary Simon have a grandson?"

"I don't think so."

I began to realize that this trip wasn't going to go fast. "Do you think I could talk to her in the hospital?"

CHAPTER FOURTEEN

Mary Simon looked at me through half-closed eyes. Bruises colored her face; her lips looked parched and swollen. Given her fragile condition, getting in to see her here at Harper Hospital could have been a trick. But Father Zerba had worked some magic. They knew him and agreed to let us visit for a few minutes. But we had to wait nearly an hour before they finally let us into the Critical Care Unit.

The priest now sat in a chair at the head of the patient's bed, leaning close, a hand touching the woman's brow. She seemed happy to see him, but every so often she glanced my way. Machines stood nearby, some attached to her, some not. They made sucking, hissing sounds. She had a rosary wrapped in her hands, her lips mouthing silent prayers.

Bob waited in a nearby TV room, sulking. He didn't like it that I wouldn't let him go with Dezi, who insisted on the way here that we leave her near a small party store on Jefferson Avenue near Old Town's riverfront warehouse district. She said she had to talk to a man named Oscar.

Zerba had a calm, compassionate manner, clearly perfected over years of sitting at bedsides. As he talked to her softly, I tried to listen in. But the sound of the machines prevented that. So I settled back in my chair for a while, thinking about Dezi resolutely making for that party store to see Oscar. I felt guilty, wondering if I was letting her go into the lion's den.

Then, speaking of guilt, I thought about Monica. I should call her.

Zerba finally turned to me. "It sounds like they're one and the same, which is what I thought. It's her nephew. His name was Donny Johnson."

"He's Native American?"

"It's a complicated story, and I'm not sure I fully understand it." Zerba now wore slacks and a baggy wool sweater over his Roman collar. "But, yes, he's Indian, and a bad actor. Sounds like he is a bit of an activist, too. Always getting into fights over Indian rights."

Mary Simon looked to be in her late sixties. Even that old and with all of the bruises, her features—firm cheekbones, proud mouth and chin—made me think she must have been a beauty at one time. But etched on that face as well were years of worry and pain.

"She says it's for the best he died, that he was stupid and evil. She says Satan had him. I think, among other things, he was into drugs."

"He was the one who beat her?"

Zerba nodded.

"Why?"

"He thought she had something that he wanted."

"What was that?"

Zerba talked to her again, quietly. "A document of some kind."

"A map?"

Again, they spoke, and I saw her shaking her head. "She doesn't know."

"That's why he beat her up?"

"Yes."

I stared at her, wondering about her life and wanting to know more. I also thought of asking what she knew about that Geronimo tattoo that her nephew wore.

But Bob appeared at the door, his large shoulders slumped, a gloomy look on his face. He might have lost his only friend. I stood and went over to him, wondering how he got into this closed unit. I told him we were almost done. Just before leaving the truck, Dezi had pecked his cheek and patted his head. "Wish me luck," she had said.

Zerba stood, one hand holding the woman's. She was crying now, silently. "She wants us to pray for her nephew's soul."

93

We circled the bed, Bob at the foot, me on one side and Zerba on the other. Bob clasped his hands over his stomach and began moving his jaw side to side, as if testing to see how loose he could make it.

"Let's have a moment of silence, and then say the Our Father."

I closed my eyes and listened to the Catholic clergyman recite the Lord's Prayer and a handful of Hail Mary's. These were prayers my mother said every night, usually behind the door of her bedroom. My Protestant father would pretend to ignore it and plunge deeper into his newspaper or Bible. The Blessed Mother, you see, is a sore spot for Protestants. Some Catholics, some of my brethren believe, worship her as if she was a feminine God.

The priest and the woman exchanged a few more words after the prayers. She spoke slowly. Again, I couldn't hear.

Outside in the hall, Zerba said he'd stick around and try to talk to her some more. "I think there's more she isn't saying."

"Like what?"

"I don't understand this document business, and then—she told me this on Sunday after she got hurt—she knows someone broke into her house last week."

"Her nephew?"

"Maybe, but she told me that she thought he came to her house this weekend straight from jail in Florida."

"He was in jail, what for?"

"She thinks for drunk driving."

"Where in Florida?"

He motioned me off to the side. We left Bob in the hallway and stepped into a little nook by another patient's room. "I think her nephew left this document with her before he took off for Florida. He came back to get it. But at first she wouldn't give it to him."

"Why?"

"I'm not sure. I think she felt it would get him into trouble if he took it."

"Did she say anything about a map of some sort?"

"I need to ask her again."

94

"It doesn't make sense, unless he was going to tell me about this map—if it somehow ties into that girl's death."

"Which is another thing," said Zerba.

I waited as he leaned close. "She told me that Donny had a girlfriend in Grand Rapids who died as few months ago."

"You're kidding!" I knew my voice had carried, but I didn't care. "Did she have a name for the girlfriend?"

"Look, Reverend, there's more here, like I say. Let me talk to her some more after she gets some rest."

Other rooms ran both ways down the hall. A couple doctors stood talking at the nearby nurses' station. A hush filled the critical-care area.

I suddenly noticed Bob peeking in the woman's room. Checking on her, maybe. In his own way, he had a big heart for the sick and lowly.

Father Zerba rested against a wall and stuck a finger inside his Roman collar. It seemed to be pinching him.

Recalling the autopsy room in Grand Rapids, I asked: "Father, when you can, can you ask her about a tattoo that her nephew had on his arm—or did she mention a tattoo of Geronimo?"

This perked him right up, and I explained what I knew and what I'd seen.

"Are you sure?"

Suddenly, from near the old woman's room came a loud voice. "Father! Who is that man and what is he doing?"

I stepped to the doorway of Mary Simon's room and saw Bob standing on the side of the patient's bed. His head was bent and his arms were raised over his head. Mary Simon gazed at him with a kind of soft wonder.

"He's praying for her recovery," I told the nurse.

The nurse had frizzy red hair, a square face and freckles. "Get him out of here."

I stepped in and touched his shoulder, hearing him mumble words. "Hey, Oral Roberts, it's time to go. We need to pick up Dezi."

Thirty minutes later, we were pulling down Jefferson, rolling past auto parts places, a fancy new marina development and businesses with accordion gates protecting their windows. A few people passed on the sidewalks. A man pushed a shopping cart bulging with his belongings. Big billboards advertised the new gambling casinos that had come to town. One of them—going up in Greektown—rose in my rearview mirror. It was a massive glittering structure, bursting with neon even in the afternoon. I hated how gambling had come to be seen as the saving grace for communities, large and small. It was like a curse, a scourge, an easy way out that only led to a continued destruction of our morals. If I sound petty and right-wing on this, so be it. Gambling too often led to addiction, and addiction always took you further from God. But then, casinos offered jobs. They offered a kind of salvation for a people that our nation had treated worse than rottenly. I yanked my brain away from these thoughts when I spotted a familiar form.

"There we are," I said to Bob when I spotted Dezi leaning against an abandoned storefront a half block from the party store. She wore her coat and smoked a cigarette.

She looked up impassively and swung away from the building as I pulled to the curb. The tattoos on her legs reminded me of fancy pantyhose.

Bob didn't move as Dezi opened the door of my truck and peered in. Instead, Monica's brother watched as a fly beat itself silly against the inside of the windshield. "Hey, Slugger," she said, gently pushing his shoulder. "Move over."

Bob did as he was asked.

Dezi's hair was a mess, pulled back and tied with a cloth. Her skin looked scrubbed of makeup in some places; it was smeared in spots around her mouth. She looked worn out.

I didn't leave right away. "Are you OK?" I asked.

"Fine."

Traffic shot by, headed north out of town. The late afternoon sun, starting to make its move toward the west, was not doing much to brighten this street. I noticed a handful of teens gathered outside the grocery. Wearing oversized, athletic clothing, they were trying to look tough and doing a pretty good job of it. I knew I needed to swing back downtown to pick up the freeway home. At this rate, we wouldn't be in Grand Rapids until after dark. Definitely, I needed to call Monica, as well as Manny. One would be probably be happy to hear from me, but not the other.

"Oscar wants to talk to you," Dezi said to me.

She apparently meant the man she had just spent the afternoon with. "What about?"

Dezi finished her cigarette and shoved the butt through a space in the window. Bob kept following the fly as it buzzed against the window.

"What does he want?" I said, getting irritated, not wanting to make any more unscheduled stops.

Dezi gave me a quick glance, still not offering much by way of expression. "Forget it."

Bob slapped the dashboard, cupping the fly and sticking it in his mouth.

"Cute," said Dezi.

Bob kept a hand over his mouth; maybe making sure it didn't escape.

"Does he do this often?" she asked.

"What?"

"Eat insects."

"Only when he's sulking."

"Big guy, that's sick," Dezi said, running her palm against the side of his face. I saw him relax and smile a little. I think his prayers had worked a little magic on the grandmother; Dezi's touch did the same to him.

"Dumb cluck," he replied, swallowing the fly..

"Your not so dumb. You just have bad habits," said Dezi.

"Super size!"

That broke the ice, and I wondered if I should talk to Oscar.

Maybe he could help fill in the blanks. After all, I assumed he had been the one who led Dezi to Mary Simon.

But Oscar didn't want to talk at his store. He wanted to meet on Belle Isle, an island park not too far down Jefferson. He told Dezi he'd be there in an hour.

"We're supposed to wait until six o'clock?" I asked.

"That's what he said."

"Why does he want to do this at Belle Isle?"

"You'll have to ask him."

I really was ticked having to wait. I was more than ready to drive home, but I decided to stick around, thinking it might be important that we talk.

So, I called Monica. I had to leave a message. Then we drove to a Burger King for an early dinner. Over Whoppers and fries, I pumped Dezi for more on Oscar, but she didn't offer much. I did sense, though, that she had not gone to see him willingly. All of my instincts told me to forget about this meeting and hightail it back to Grand Rapids. But another part of me said to stay.

As Dezi and Bob shared apple pie, I called Manny and got another answering machine.

Finally, just before 6 p.m., we were back on Jefferson, headed for Belle Isle.

Just past the site of a former tire plant, now a huge area of redevelopment, I turned down the road leading to the low-slung General Douglas MacArthur Bridge—site of big race riot in 1943. My mother had told me about it. The fighting and violence broke out just as she and friends were leaving after spending the day at a picnic. This is the same bridge from which magician Harry Houdini was thrown, it being winter, through a hole in the ice in a locked trunk. He escaped his chains, only to be unable to find the hole in the ice. He had to bob and swim along the air space between the water and ice until he could find safety. I was feeling a little like that—floating in a chilly uncertain space, just this side of fear, wondering what would happen next. "Where am I going?" I asked.

"He said by the big fountain."

The Detroit River flowed below as we crossed the bridge and the city's skyline spread to our right. Canada, a more modest urban sprawl, was straight ahead.

"Dezi," I said, "did Oscar mention anything about a map of some kind?"

"Of what?"

"No."

Bob grinned like a happy pumpkin, one of Dezi's hands clutched in his.

"Who is Oscar, really?" I said.

Dezi turned slowly, looking around Bob. The tip of her nose was red and leaky. She wiped under it with the back of a hand. "Why?"

"Did he hurt you today?" I asked.

She sniffed again, but didn't answer.

Traffic wasn't too bad. "How does Oscar know so much?" I wondered.

"Ask him."

Dezi nodded at a small, chubby man in a black jogging suit who stepped out of a black Lexus parked in a small lot near a red Hummer. The ornate fountain, now turned off, sat on our left.

As I pulled in, Oscar raised his arms over his head, and a slice of his white belly came into view. He looked to be in his fifties. I'd lay money he had not been jogging.

I parked between the Lexus and the Hummer. Oscar scowled and wiped a hand over his face as I rolled down my window.

Dezi got out, leaving the door open, and addressed him over the roof of my Ranger. "This is the preacher from Grand Rapids."

He had tiny nervous eyes and yellow and black running shoes tied on his feet.

Oscar gave me the once-over. His tongue appeared and licked the side of his mouth. Chunks of what looked like potato chips specked the front of his jogging jacket. He scratched his belly. He was a real piece of work. "How do you know Dolores?"

"Dolores?"

"Her," he answered, pointing his pudgy finger at Dezi.

"I was wondering the same thing about you," I answered, climbing out. Bob had squeezed next to Dezi.

Oscar looked up as I unfolded myself from the seat. Despite his sloppy demeanor, I saw sharpness on his face, a quick ability to size things up. "Her and me go way back," he answered and grinned.

"She says you want to talk."

"Not me." He dug behind an ear. "Them."

A man in a long black leather jacket appeared from the front of the Hummer. He had a hard, long face, small eyes and a Mohawk haircut. Another man rounded the rear. He was well built, beard-stubbled, black-haired and wore a cut-off sweatshirt that showed big steroid biceps. Stupid, I told myself, thinking I should have paid closer attention to that boxy vehicle being parked so close to us.

"You done with me?" Oscar called over to Mohawk.

"You're driving," Mohawk answered, grabbing Dezi by the arm and yanking her toward him. I saw a small semi-automatic handgun in his hand. Mr. Steroid—he reminded me of Arnold, California's movie-star governor—eyed Bob like he was going to eat him for dinner.

We were between the Hummer and my truck, hidden by a leafy hedge. Cars slipped by on the road. But no one was looking. This was a nice park island, but it still was Detroit.

"Stop messing around, let's go," said Mohawk. He stuck the gun to Dezi's head.

Bob started for him. But he had to slip by me. So I held him back, noticing scars crisscrossing Mohawk's face.

Bob shoved hard to get by. "No, big guy," Dezi said, one eye looking for the barrel at her skull. "Better do what they say."

Mohawk meanwhile hooked an arm around her neck. The weapon, in his other hand, touched her temple.

"Both of you in the van. Now," Mohawk said to Bob and me.

I stayed where I was.

"What about the whore?" asked Arnold.

"She goes with Fatso."

"Hey, that wasn't in the deal," whined Oscar.

I stepped forward. "What's this about?"

"Someone wants to talk to you," said Mohawk.

"Who?"

"Just get in the van and you'll see."

CHAPTER FIFTEEN

Mohawk circled the island, exited the bridge and then drove north along the river to the Chrysler Freeway, which he entered and started a swing through downtown. Arnold kept me in line by—as I saw in the rear-view mirror—aiming the gun directly up Bob's nose.

I was in front; they were in back. A couple of times I asked what was going on, but they didn't answer. It was probably 7 p.m., the end of rush hour as we headed in the direction of the Ambassador Bridge, whose metal towers rose in the distance.

Finally, hearing Bob moan, I turned around.

"What're you looking at?" Arnold demanded, now training the gun at Bob's temple. Monica's brother trembled.

A jolt of rage ran through me. "If you hurt him, you muscle-bound jerk, I'll find a way to stick that gun up your ass and then pull the trigger." No way, of course, for a man of God to talk. But God wasn't here with us right now to do the talking.

Arnold replied, swinging the gun my way, "I'd love to see you try." His eyes danced with a frightening glee.

"Man, is that any way for a minister to talk?" Mohawk asked, eyes on the road.

"Who says I'm a minister?"

Mohawk chuckled.

I wondered why swearing bothered this guy so much—if it did.

"How am I supposed to talk when a pair of pinheads show up out of nowhere and force us to ride in this damned truck."

Mohawk smiled. "There you go again."

"Who are you? And what do you want?"

Mohawk turned on the radio and loud rap music filled the Hummer.

Not too long after, he left the freeway. Soon we parked alongside the large gutted shell of the Michigan Central Railroad building, the one I stared at from under the ringing bell at Zerba's church.

"Now what?" I asked.

"We wait."

Built by the same people who constructed Grand Central Station in New York City, this structure held a kind of grandeur, even in its dilapidation. I'd seen a documentary on it recently. The filmmaker referred to it as one the nation's most endangered architectural treasures. If you asked me, endangered was sugar coating it.

Light cut through many of the open windows of the once-ornate railroad depot—a huge hollow space now. Through the wide-open front entryway, I saw stripped-bare walls and the floor littered with plaster, cement and twisted metal.

When I was in there as a kid to catch a train, murals covered the walls, huge columns rose to the massive ceiling, people bustled everywhere and trains rushed in on the wind of whistles and then blasted out for parts unknown.

I recall standing on the rail siding, my mom holding one hand and my father the other. My mother loved the rush and crush of activity. My dad hated it. He stood in his farmer's jeans and jacket, grim-faced, looking like he wanted to be anywhere but there.

Mohawk pulled a ringing cell phone out of his coat pocket, popped it open, and then listened. That reminded me that my cell phone was in my truck.

After hanging up, Mohawk got the Hummer moving, half-circled the building and then pulled up to the end of a short road, where he parked near the entrance to a tunnel. He gazed over at me. "You are in for a treat, Reverend."

"What kind?"

"Someone important wants to talk to you," he said.

Parked construction vehicles and piles of sodden boxes filled the open area on either side of the Hummer. Eighteen stories of broken windows rose above us. I saw dark dots flying from a few windows.

I took them to be bats. In front of us stretched the tunnel through which, I assumed, trains once rolled. To the right was a large, gutted doorway. "So, who wants to talk?" I asked.

Mohawk tapped the steering wheel. He didn't answer.

Then the goons stepped out, ordering us after them. But I stayed put. Mohawk came over to my side, opened the door and held up his hands, as if to show me he had nothing to hide.

"Who're we meeting?"

He gazed at me with hard eyes. "Someone who wants to talk to you about who died in that church."

"You idiots had to kidnap us at gunpoint for that?"

Mohawk smiled, but it wasn't pleasant. "You are a mouthy man of God, aren't you?" He stepped to the side, making room for me to get out.

"Look," I said, climbing out, "why do we have to go in there?"

"Because that's where he wants to meet."

"Who is he?"

Mohawk didn't want to talk any more.

Once I helped Bob squeeze out, we entered the rear of the depot through a large doorway and stepped into a vast, cold and empty room. Years of neglect and vandalism had buckled the floor, caved in the ceiling, and torn many of the water-stained walls open to the studs. And this wasn't even the main terminal area.

We plodded along silently, patches of late evening sunlight showing here and there, to a staircase, up which we trudged. The stairs, given the condition of the rest of the structure, were remarkably clean and clear of crud.

I lost count at the fifth floor. My legs ached and my lungs hurt, but we kept going, floor after floor, until Mohawk shouldered me off and through an empty doorway. Bob and Arnold kept climbing. "Hey," I said, "where're they going?"

"Don't worry," Mohawk said.

"We need to stay together," I said to Mohawk.

"Move," he ordered, shoving me into a hallway. I did not like abandoning Bob. But I suspected any tricky stuff from me would lead to big problems for him. Still, I started after him, only to bump into Mohawk who shoved me hard with his chest, swung me around and pushed again. I let him.

We started walking, going by empty offices. Electrical wires hung from the ceiling. I heard birds squawking and flittering and imagined rats and other vermin sliding along the walls next to us.

Near the end of the hall we stopped, standing face to face. His eyes burned, sending out scary signals.

"I'm Muslim," he said and smiled a tight dangerous grin I could just make out in the dim light.

"What's that got to do with anything?"

"I don't lie—or swear."

"But you do carry a gun?"

Mohawk stepped close and, before I could react, pressed the weapon into my belly and I knew this was it. But it wasn't.

"Inside there," he said. " He'll be here in awhile."

"Who?" I asked.

"Inside."

"Is Bob safe?"

Mohawk jerked his head, wanting me to stop fooling around.

"I need to know that muscle-brained fool isn't going to shoot him."

"Shut up." He shoved me through the doorway so hard that I stumbled and nearly fell.

Maybe an hour went by. I was now standing at the open window and letting my eyes wander the lights several floors below. They winked and sparkled, spreading in haphazard strings toward the even greater dazzle of downtown, in the midst of which shown the lights of the Greektown casino.

Almost directly below, beyond the reach of the central city with its new casinos and soaring skyscrapers, spread a less startling perspective. Streetlights lit the landscape, but much of it remained dark. Downriver Detroit, Zug Island, and the edge of Dearborn and the suburb of Taylor sprawled out there—a wasteland of empty homes, abandoned industry and lives lost to the terror of the city.

For some reason I thought of lyrics from an old Bob Dylan song, from his Blonde on Blonde album, "The ghosts of electricity howl in the bones of her face." Detroit seemed like that to me—a ghost of its former self, its power hidden amid broken neighborhoods and industrial zones left to rot.

I walked away from the window to peer through a crack in the door to see Mohawk still keeping guard in the hall, a silent sentry, hardly moving in his black coat.

I then paced the drafty room, as I had been doing before standing at the window, wondering where they had taken Bob. Dezi, I assumed, was with Oscar. Monica, I was sure, was going through the roof with worry.

Finally, as I returned to the window, I heard voices in the hall and shoes scraping the floor. I turned, feeling the breeze come through the open window behind me and nudge the back of my neck.

The door opened and two shadows stood there. Mohawk was one; the other man I didn't recognize.

The one I didn't know said something to Mohawk, who retreated and shut the door. Things were almost totally dark now. I heard a snap and saw the flare of a match. As he lit a smoke, I caught a mustache, a thick thatch of hair and wide neck. Then the match died and only the orange tip and a cigar smell remained.

He emerged slowly out of the shadows, moving my way and coming to a stop maybe three feet from where I stood. He held out a hand. "I'm Jamal."

We shook. His hand was warm, wet and thick. But he squeezed lightly. I saw his eyes sparkle, his forehead wide and softly lined. He wore a tailored suit, shiny shoes, and had a mouth that made me think of an oyster—hard, large and slimy.

"You are the minister from Grand Rapids, I am right?"

"How come everyone knows me?"

Then he stepped closer, facing the window. He smoked reflectively

106

for a bit, tendrils from his cigar sifting out into the night. Behind me I heard a snap, bump and fast fluttering. Several black balls shot overhead, whizzing by our heads, cruising into the evening sky. I watched them go.

"Do you like bats, my friend?"

"What kind of question is that?"

"People hate bats, but they do a very good job of eating other bugs—bugs that can make you sick."

"You brought me here to talk public health?"

His mean mouth registered a smile. A half moon, riding high above Motown, threw milky light on us, sketching his face and body with a delicate outline, a soft aura that I suspected belied the truth.

"This building, my friend, the city wants to tear it down. What do you think?" Jamal asked.

I didn't answer, wondering where this was headed.

I shrugged.

"Do you like it, this old railroad building. It has much history, or so they say."

"What's not to like—bats, garbage, maniacs in leather coats."

Something slid into his eyes. Maybe it was a warning. Whatever, he seemed to decide to get down to business. "I'm sorry the way you were treated."

"My friend, Bob, how is he?"

Jamal raised a hand, as if telling me not to interrupt. "I want you to accept my apologies for how this has happened."

"Then we can go?" The empty space behind me felt vast. I heard a siren and the rush of tires and grinding of engines.

"When we are finished, yes."

"What do you want?"

He smoked, the tip flaring. "So, tell me..." The cigar burned bright a second before he dropped it to the floor and crushed it out with his shoe. "Why did that slut bring you here?"

"I assume you mean Dezi."

"She's a whore, you know?"

107

"Do you mind telling me who you are?"

He faced me, starting to give off very bad vibes. "Why are you in Detroit?"

"A young man died in Grand Rapids. As a minister, I came to tell the relatives what happened."

"You came a long way to do that."

"Oh, it was a pretty short drive."

Silence. The air grew colder. Earlier I had examined random graffiti scrawled over the walls of this room that at one time was probably someone's office.

Jamal took in a deep breath and let it out. Outside, St. Anne's bells started in, bonged out nine and then shut down..

"Tell me about Mary Simon," he said.

"Why?"

Jamal reached up and wiped something off my shoulder. It was a quick, almost gentle gesture. "Please," he said. "I know now the slut was lying. So you are in no danger. She had told us things, but they…" He gestured with his hand, as if dismissing Dezi's words. "They aren't truth. Please, talk to me about Mrs. Simon. Tell me what you know about her nephew Don."

He knew the names. He was also telling me that Dezi was a double-crosser. "You know her nephew?"

Jamal turned back to the widow, gazing out with his hands behind his back. "I am a businessman here. I know lots of people."

I looked outside as well, spotting the flipping blue lights of a police cruiser zipping along a street near the church.

"What kind of business are you in?" I asked.

"That doesn't matter."

"I don't really know much."

He faced me and spread his hands apart, as if showing me the size of a fish he had caught. "You tell what you know. Then your friend upstairs and you can go back to Grand Rapids."

"What if what I know is not very blessed much?"

"Please, my friend, let me be the judge of that."

CHAPTER SIXTEEN

Father Zerba met us at the door of his rectory, a pair of tied-to-gether boxing gloves looped over a shoulder, and waved us in.

Just as Jamal promised, Bob met me outside the room once we finished talking and, having been left to our own devices by Mohawk and his boss, followed me down the stairs and outside. We headed straight here.

After I filled Zerba in, he asked if we were hungry. He offered to heat up meat loaf, but I settled for a peanut butter sandwich and chips and asked to use the phone. As he led Bob into the kitchen, I stepped into a side room to make my calls.

Neither Manny nor Monica answered and so I left messages, giving each a very brief rundown on the day.

A few minutes later in the dining room, I sipped coffee as Bob wolfed down his third bowl of Honey Nut Cheerios. Zerba sat at the head of the table, drinking a beer.

Bent over and shoveling it in, Monica's brother looked like a big kid. Hungry as I was, I didn't eat much. The remains of my late dinner sat in front of me on the table. Staring at the sandwich and chips, I found it hard to believe I stood in that dingy room less than an hour before. But our problems weren't over.

While Jamal had let us go, my truck was still missing, as was Dezi.

"Do you want something else to eat, Reverend?"

"Getting kidnapped spoiled my appetite."

The rangy priest took a pull on the bottle of beer, letting the liquid fill his mouth, where he kept it a moment, as if reflecting, and then swallowed. He had set the boxing gloves on the table next to him. He had already explained that he'd been at the nearby Roberto

Clemente Recreation Center, teaching kids how to fight, until just before we showed up from the railroad building.

We came here because I had no idea where else to go. Jamal and I had had a relatively friendly discussion, considering the circumstances.

"You know," I said, nodding at Zerba's beer, "maybe I'll have one."

He shoved away from the table and went after it.

This dining room smelled musty and underused. Maybe that's how rectories always smelled; I hadn't been in enough of them to know. Plates showing the faces of saints with bright halos were displayed atop a tall mahogany cabinet, across from me and behind Bob. "How're you holding up?" I asked Monica's brother.

He stopped eating long enough to raise his fists and smile at the gloves by the priest's empty chair. I was so relieved he was safe, and guilty that I had gotten us into a situation I still didn't understand. But he seemed no worse for the wear.

Zerba returned with a can of beer and set it by my coffee cup. He also had a plate of cookies, which he stuck between us. Bob snatched two. Taking his seat, the priest cradled the beer in his large hands and gave me a very long and serious look.

Munching cookies, Bob went for my brew. Truthfully, the last thing I needed was liquor. But he didn't either, so I grabbed it back. This made him fold his arms over his chest and blow out his lips. I left the can unopened.

We were quiet awhile. A clock ticked somewhere; electricity seemed to hum gently in the walls. I thought of the Dylan song again. Also, I noticed a picture of Jesus and his mother were framed in a photo on the wall behind the priest. Palms fronds were stuck behind it. Seeing Jesus offered me comfort.

But my mind was still stuck on what had happened. Then, as if trying to get it unstuck, I hit the table with my hand. "At least they could have brought my truck back."

Both Bob and priest looked at me like I was a nut—and at that moment I probably was.

"I'll take to you Belle Isle to get it," said Zerba.

"I doubt that it's there. The one with the Mohawk said to Oscar that he was supposed to drive it."

"Let's find Oscar."

But I hoped to hear from Manny before heading off, assuming he could advise me on what to do about Jamal, on whether to call the local cops or let it ride for the time being. Then, there was Dezi. Should I leave her, or try to track her down, too?

Bob reached for the beer again, sort of sneaky. I let him have it. He popped the top and took a big foamy gulp.

"Exactly who is Jamal?" I asked the priest.

Zerba drank his own beer, tilting away from the light and checking a window by the cabinet.

"He's got a hand in everything. He develops real estate, runs a chain of party stores and other things. But his biggest deal is his stake in one of the big gambling casinos downtown."

"Which one?"

"The MGM, I think?"

"He owns it?"

"I'm not sure. Did he talk to you about it?"

I nodded. "He seemed to know a lot about the plans for a casino up our way."

Zerba picked up one of his boxing gloves, turned it over and wiped something off a place by the wrist pad. The priest gave me a weary smile. "What did he say?"

"He asked a lot of questions."

The priest leaned back in his chair. "Jamal is a dangerous man."

"Do you know him personally?"

"We've spoken a time or two."

"I'm wondering, Father, did you get a chance to ask Mary Simon any more about that map?"

"A little."

"And?"

"I need to talk to her again."

111

A map of some kind clearly stuck in many people's minds.

"But she did know of one?" I asked.

Zerba held up his hand. "Possibly."

"Jamal mentioned one."

Zerba's face registered interest. "What did he say?"

"Only that Donny Johnson had it, or so he thought."

"Who does he think has it now?"

"He didn't say."

My attention turned to Bob who had taken a wadded handkerchief out of somewhere. With great fanfare, he dabbed his face, then set it down, unwrapped the handkerchief and started poking around in it.

I reached over to grab it, tired of his antics. Then I felt something inside. I unwadded the cloth, spread it on the table, finding a ring of some sort. Purple dots that looked like blood speckled the material.

"Where'd you get this?" I demanded.

His face drew a blank.

I held it up, saw some kind of inscription on the side, around an inlaid, ruby cross.

"Whose is this?"

"Dezi," Bob then said, slapping both hands on the table, his voice trembling. "Dezi!" he repeated for the entire rectory to hear.

"It's hers?" I asked.

We both stared at him.

"Dezi," he said again.

"She gave you the ring?" I asked.

Bob's face was getting red, as if heat built up inside. Suddenly his large jaw set. "Dezi,'" he said defiantly.

"She gave it to you?"

"No!" he roared.

Zerba looked at me for an explanation, but I didn't have one.

Bob was mad; it sometimes comes on him fast, these thunder-clouds rolling into his disordered mind. "What about Dezi" I asked, trying to talk softer.

Either she gave it to him, or somehow the ring connected in his

112

head with her being gone. Maybe he found it in the railroad building and for some reason it fired his brain to think of her.

Bob had his arms folded over his chest again.

"Dezi may have sold us down the river, partner," I told him.

No matter to Bob.

Zerba reached over and edged the handkerchief toward him. "Is this blood?" He pointed at the speck.

"It sure looks like it."

Bob stood, threw over his chair, and yelled, "Dezi!"

As we looked at him, the phone rang in the other room. Zerba checked me out and I nodded for him to answer it.

Once the priest left the room, Bob eyes flooded with tears. "Dezi," he said more softly.

I examined the handkerchief, trying to think of something, but not sure what. I stepped close, put my arm around him and let him cry.

Twenty minutes later, we rode along I-94, zipping east across town through sparse traffic. Expressway lights threw down a faint yellow glow.

Bob sat in the back of Zerba's Tracker, quiet and attentive. Downtown loomed straight ahead as we rode by the dark form of Tiger Stadium, the baseball park now in mothballs. Detroit's baseball team played these days in a new stadium named after a bank.

It had been Manny on the phone. Before leaving, I gave him a quick rundown on the day's events, including discovery of the ring in what looked to be a bloodstained handkerchief, which, Manny asked me to check for a monogram. There was none. Like me, he figured it came from the railroad building, but he said to hang onto it. Then he said I would be best heading home and leave Dezi to her own devices. He also said he would talk to a friend on the Detroit Police Department about Jamal. I could make a report on him tonight, but maybe it would be best, given all that was going on, that I leave things to the authorities. We would talk when we got back. But, first, I had to locate my truck.

113

Well, that wasn't so easy, as it turned out. We tried Belle Isle without any luck.

We rode around the island twice, hoping to spot it, to no avail. We even flagged down a cop and asked him if he'd seen a black Ford Ranger ditched somewhere. He hadn't and asked if we wanted to report it stolen. I asked if he could take down the information, and he said I would have to make the report in person at the local precinct house. So I decided to pass, asking the priest to take us back to that party store that Oscar apparently owned.

Zerba left the island and started south on Jefferson, retracing our steps. I thought of calling Manny again, but decided to hold off. Instead, I asked the priest, "You said you did talk a little more to Mrs. Simon?"

Zerba cleared his throat, as if getting ready to address the crowd, then said, "I think she hid a copy of this map in her apartment."

"Is it still there?"

"I think so."

Shadows from the other side of the freeway rolled over the priest. "She says it was some kind of map to a place, a camp of some kind that her nephew kept by a river... She also said that..." He paused, and went on. "Donny and his girlfriend in Grand Rapids had gotten into some kind of fight."

"Was her name Melinda?"

"I didn't ask."

"When was this?"

"Back in February."

"That's when Melinda was killed!"

Zerba nodded.

"What else did she say?"

"A doctor came in at that point and chased me out. I can try again tomorrow."

"We need to ask her about the map."

Curlicues of concrete, exits and entrance ramps rose above us. Lights winked in a few of the towering office buildings. This map was important.

114

"Maybe the police need to talk to Mary Simon," Zerba said.

"Maybe."

Jefferson ran along the river, shooting past blank storefronts, a Church of Christ building and a large, brightly illuminated gas station. I was trying to figure out the map, but something else nagged me, and it wasn't Dezi or my lost truck. But I couldn't quite figure what it was.

I looked at the priest, whose big hands were flexing on the steering wheel. His nose, in profile, was slightly flat. If I had to be with someone in an area like this at midnight, I was glad it was with him. "How long've you been boxing?" I asked.

"Longer than I've been a priest."

"There it is," I said, spotting Oscar's grocery store ahead. People milled out front. Earlier, I hadn't noticed the sign: Jefferson Grab 'n' Go. It stood there in a hazy yellow light, the only open business for a couple blocks. Not far away was the corner at which I'd picked Dezi up from earlier.

Zerba slowed and turned into the parking lot, half full with cars and trucks. We scattered a couple teens as we rolled in. They didn't like having to move, but Zerba gave them no choice.

He parked near the back. "I'll go in," he said. "I think I know the kid who works nights here. His dad goes to St. Lazar's."

"You think he's working now?"

"I'll soon see."

"We'll come with you."

"No, I'll be right back."

We watched him go, heading straight for a pack of young kids, many clad in over-sized sweatshirts and shiny warm-up jackets. He stopped to talk with them. A couple got mouthy, but soon things settled down, and they all spoke civilly for a few moments. Then Zerba made for the store, his long legs taking him there in a hurry. A couple of the kids, the mouthy ones, peered our way.

"Well, Bob, where do you think the bad guys hid my truck?" I asked.

115

He didn't answer.

I was already thinking I'd rent a car to take him back to Grand Rapids and then, probably as early as tomorrow, return here with Manny—if my Ranger didn't show up soon. I had tried Monica again before leaving the rectory, but no dice.

Meanwhile, shadows shifted behind the priest's Tracker. I heard voices and felt the rear bumper bounce.

Bob turned and looked out the back.

I waited, not liking this at all, feeling the truck move again. Then I popped the door and got out. Chilly air touched my face. Beer signs, barely visible in the dark, fluttered and flapped from the side of the Grab 'n' Go.

"What's up, fellas?" I asked the handful of teens gathered behind Zerba's vehicle.

"Say what, Holmes?" A skinny teen swaggered my way, his entourage not far behind. He wore a painter's cap backward on his head. Bright tennis shoes, which lit up as he stepped my way, were on his feet. He stuck his hands in the side pockets of his puffy coat.

"Why are you messing with my friend's truck?" I asked.

The kid came closer, a couple feet away now, bouncing on the toes of his shoes. Others gathered. I was tired and irritable and in no mood for this. "This tall white man wants to know why we're messing with the truck. You hear that, Montel?" asked the kid in the cap.

Montel appeared out of the shadows. He looked like a miniature King Kong.

I checked over my shoulder, hoping to see the priest.

"So what brings you out here so late, white man?" asked the scrawny leader. "Are you looking for some girls?"

"Stop with the white guy business," I snapped.

Montel giggled.

The kid stepped closer to me, but then nearly fell back as Bob hopped out of the truck and immediately started hopping from foot to foot, uttering a loud growl.

"Hey, what's his problem?" asked the kid.

116

"He doesn't like you," I told the kid.

Montel edged closer, glaring at Bob. But Bob wheeled and started beating his chest. Holy Cow, I thought, now he was King Kong.

Montel reached for his pocket, but suddenly an arm appeared out of nowhere and wrapped around his neck, forcing a startled look to cross his face. Zerba had him by the throat from behind. "Who is Alonzo?" Zerba asked.

No one spoke. The priest put pressure on Montel. He started to gag. I think he wanted to turn and fight, but the priest had him good. "Who is Alonzo?" Zerba asked again.

The kid with the illuminated shoes took a few seconds, but finally admitted he was.

"We want to talk to Oscar," said the priest. "The man inside says you can take us to where he lives. He says it's in alley behind a bar, the Four Seasons."

Alonzo looked at the party store, as if checking to see if what Zerba said was right.

"Of course, we're willing to pay," said Zerba, easing away from Montel, who started to rub his neck.

"How much?" asked Alonzo.

The priest put a hand on Alonzo's shoulder. "Don't worry. It'll be worth your while."

"How much?"

"Twenty bucks."

"Make it fifty."

Zerba stepped close to Alonzo. "Twenty."

Alonzo tilted his chin in the direction of the priest. "I want Montel to come along."

We looked for Montel, but he had already started to fade away into the dark.

That answered that.

Agreeing to take a twenty, Alonzo climbed in the back with Bob. Firing up his Tracker, Zerba checked the rear-view mirror. "Buckle up."

No answer.

"I mean it," said the priest.

I heard two clicks.

A few minutes later, the priest hung a left off Jefferson, a mile or so from where we'd picked Dezi up hours before. We were about two blocks from the Detroit River in an area under development for new businesses and condos.

We wove through a few streets, heading north, toward downtown. "Where is it, Alonzo?" asked the priest.

"Next street, go left."

Zerba followed the directions.

We drove past a long dark factory, a row of equally dark houses and then, a half block up on our right, a neon sign flashed the name of a bar: the Four Seasons.

"Dezi?" asked Bob.

"We're getting close, I hope," I answered, remembering she had told me she once worked at a bar with this name.

Zerba braked and pulled up to the front of the joint. It had no windows. The front door hung open, a haze of smoke pouring from within.

Alonzo bounced on the seat. "We're here, man. This is where he hangs out. Where's my money?"

"Does he live here or hang out in the bar?" asked Zerba.

"Both. He lives around back, behind the bar, at the top of a bunch of stairs. His door is, like, painted with stripes," said Alonzo.

"How can I be sure?" asked Zerba,

"Man, I ain't lying. Gimme the money."

So we paid him and he slipped out, pulling a cell phone out of his pocket to make a call. I watched his small frame disappear down the block.

Bob was getting antsy.

"What's Oscar look like?" asked Zerba.

I gave him a description, and the priest suggested we check in the bar before knocking on his door. "If he's in the bar, maybe it would be easier."

"You want me to go in?" I asked.

The priest shrugged. I wondered if he'd hit his limit of helping out.

Bob walked next to me as we entered the bar. Sound from a Bob Seger song blasted our way. Two topless dancers swayed atop a large table, around which four or five men sat, staring at the women with a strange mixture of desire and dismay.

For a flash of a moment, I thought one of dancers was Dezi. She wore only a black G-string and had reddish-blonde hair. Her breasts were large and glossy. She had no tattoos. The other woman was black and skinny and had eyes peering from the bottom of a pit.

Bob stared with his mouth agape.

I was about to step in farther when a large man emerged from our right. He was about my height, but carrying at least 100 more pounds of flesh, a good portion of which looked like muscle. "There's a cover charge," he said.

He had dark hair, huge forearms and wore a T-shirt cut off at the sleeves. "Is Oscar around?" I had to nearly shout over the bang and bash of rock music. Seger's voice held a rhythm the women vaguely followed.

"Who's asking?" the big man asked.

"We're friends," I said. "He told us to stop by if we were in town."

Bob started to walk in, but I held him back.

The guy, clearly the bouncer, gave me a hard once over. "He's gone," he finally said, and the music died for a second.

Rows of colored bottles sat on shelves behind the bar. The bartender was a woman, also in the buff, who had platinum blonde hair. But I saw no one who looked like the chubby guy I met at Belle Isle.

"Will he be back?" I asked.

"Not tonight."

"He lives upstairs?" I asked.

"Who're you again?"

A couple of the guys at the table were now talking to the dancers, neither of whom paid them much mind. Both seemed either profoundly bored or stoned, or both.

119

Another song started. Billy Joel began singing about Catholic girls starting much too late.

"Are you in or out?" growled the bouncer.

Both dancers climbed down from the table and joined two men on their chairs. A lap dance is what I took it to be, and turned away, ashamed of myself for being here. "Buddy?" The bouncer gave me a friendly shove.

It was enough to send Bob into action. He slipped by, going for the bouncer's neck with both hands. The guy stumbled back, grabbing for something on a stool.

I stepped in front of Monica's brother. "Thanks," I said to the guy, who had picked up a club. He glowered, his eyes nearly crossed, those arms rippling with fat and muscle. He wanted to smack someone, but we were out of there.

A maze of wooden stairways climbed to the tops of flat-roofed warehouse apartments. A hazy sky hung overhead. A sense of utter desolation, a feeling of brokenness I found hard to explain, started to nag me as we pulled down the alley and stopped. Mesmerized by the images of the dancers, those men back there had seemed so vulnerable. Their lust was palpable and so sad.

But there was some good news. I spotted my truck next to a dumpster. I hopped out, and gave it a quick inspection. Everything seemed to be intact. The keys, though, were nowhere to be had.

"This must be the place,'" said Zerba, stepping next to me.

"Should we try the apartment?" I asked.

"It's up to you."

"I need my keys."

The priest led the way, making the rickety wooden stairs creak and pop. As we climbed higher, I caught the city's late-night pace—a steady tread of tires, the chugging of machines, and the muffled mix of human voices, sounding far off, protected by walls. And under it all—a constant thumping, like blood pounding from a heart, the music from the bar, the clinking of machines, of tumblers moving, of people hoping. Nearby, a dog started howling.

We reached the third floor. I felt a cold rush of wind up here. The door in front of us was indeed painted with stripes. As Zerba knocked, Bob stepped behind me.

I heard a voice inside, a low rumble.

Zerba knocked again.

"Who's there?"

"Father Frank Zerba, a priest at Saint Lazar's."

"I don't want any."

The priest pounded the door again.

"Go away, save some other souls."

I thought that I recognized the voice. "Oscar, I need the keys to my truck."

He swore at me.

I tried the knob of the door and felt it move. I looked at the priest, who shrugged and nodded.

I gave the door my shoulder and it flew open, slamming into Oscar, forcing him to stumble, trip and come to rest with his butt on a table. A small, fat, disheveled man with a hairy, heavy-breasted chest, he wore Bermuda shorts and held a phone to his belly. He started to bring it to his mouth, but Zerba grabbed it.

"Hey!" Oscar yelled.

A light behind him showed the way down a hall. Bob trundled that way. I went after him. I heard Oscar swearing and demanding what we wanted.

Dezi lay on a mattress in a dingy room without a window. I had to peer around Bob to see her. A light fixture, attached to a chain, dangled from the ceiling above her. She looked bruised and beaten. A dirty blanket covered her upper body. The room stank of vomit and stale booze. Black ash sat in a pile near her head, the remains of someone smoking, and not cigarettes.

Squeezing past Bob, I sank to my knees on the floor. Rock music thumped from the bar below. The dancers were probably atop the tables. The bouncer was likely wondering who we were. I'd bet it had been him on the phone, which made me think we had to make it quick.

I touched Dezi's forehead. It felt cold and rubbery. She turned her puffy face toward me. "Is that the big guy there with you?" she asked after a moment.

Bob knelt next to me.

The music downstairs grew louder. Dezi's face was lumpy; her eyes dull, her expression lifeless.

"Can you move?" I asked Dezi.

One of her hands rose and grabbed for Bob's fingers, snagging one and squeezing.

This close I saw the ridge of broken blood vessels along the side of her chin; matted hair; an ugly welt by her temple. I noticed dried blood on the mattress where her head had been before we showed. "What happened?" I asked.

"Oscar likes to party."

Bob sat on the floor and kept her hand in his.

"He gets off hurting people," she added.

Drums surged below, throttling the floor, voices rising. I thought of Monica, beaten once and in a hospital room. I thought of other women I had ministered to in the aftermath of a beating. Then there were those to whom I'd tended as a paramedic. Some with broken teeth; one with a gash the size of an apple in her leg.

Zerba showed up in the doorway, his long shadow falling over the bed. He stared hard at Dezi. "We need to leave."

"C'mon," I said to Dezi.

She spoke with weak conviction. "I should stay."

I stood, feeling the downstairs music rise like new life in my blood. The yelp of horns, the driving tempo of the drums filled me and fueled my anger. I knew she had probably betrayed us, but I suspected Oscar had pushed her into it. "Help her get up," I said, shoving past Zerba.

Oscar didn't turn as I entered the kitchen. But he knew I was there. Beer cans littered the room. Finally, he glanced over his shoulder at me. "What're you looking at?" he asked, holding a bottle of vodka in one hand.

"At a fat pervert."

Pockmarks dotted the flabby nape of his neck.

"Why did you do that to her?"

He sneered. "She likes it."

I forgot I was a minister. I forgot my turn-the-other-cheek training. I ignored the words of Christ who called on us to make peace, not to tear others to pieces. I shoved out of my mind the reality that if you cross a certain line, you become as bad as those you hate. I stepped over, grabbed the booze bottle from Oscar's hands and flung it toward a small tower of dishes in the sink. Glass crashed and broke, which felt good. Leaning down, I stuck my face even with his. "Where are the keys to my truck, you turd?"

He heaved up, moving for me. I gave him a forearm to the chin. He twisted, slumped and fell back, blood spurting from his mouth. Watching him squirm and bleed, I felt awful, realizing I had just dishonored my calling. But I wanted to pay him back. Jesus had chased out the money changers, and this man was worse, much worse.

Then the door burst open and Mr. Bouncer appeared, club in hand, violence in his eyes. He started for me, but the priest intervened.

The bouncer swung the club in his direction, but Zerba stepped deftly to the side and gave him a powerful uppercut, sending him against a wall, where he slumped, dazed, blood pouring from his nose.

"No, big guy. Don't! Put me down!"

Bob appeared with Dezi over his shoulder. She wasn't putting up much fight.

"You whore, you bitch!" yelled Oscar, stumbling to his feet, starting for her.

I gave him another forearm.

The bouncer started to come to life.

I looked around, spotted my keys on the table by some beer cans. I grabbed them and we left.

CHAPTER SEVENTEEN

The dream had me walking toward Brother Terry Blanton, a dwarf standing on a stool. An angry, spirit-filled minister, he had plagued my dreams before. The tent revivalist midget had scoured my soul in real life many years before. During a dusky service at the small airport in Plainwell, Blanton convinced me of my teenage sinfulness. His words brought me stumbling, along with the others, down that hay-strewn aisle, toward the salvation he offered me through Christ.

Again, I walked the aisle, but it seemed to have no end. The harder I tried, the further away it seemed to grow. Unable to make it with the others to the altar where a new life awaited, I could see the midget's twisted face, the fire in the stubby man's eyes, and the spit flying from his mouth. I knew he could provide what I needed. He was a furnace of faith, waiting to consume me, and I wanted what he had.

Then I was a paramedic again, on duty in the bowels of some science fiction city. Someone else was driving, and we were racing to get to the call. A young man was in bad trouble. He was lying in an alley. No, it was a parking lot. When we arrived, I ran to him, setting my bag on the ground. His eyes were wide, his limbs twisted, a pool of blood leaking from somewhere below his belly and staining the pavement underneath him. I reached out to help him, but he lifted up and tried to bite me. Suddenly, it was Brother Blanton again, spewing a brimstone rage, blaming me for my sins. Although I knew the bleeding kid needed help, I turned and ran—back into that ugly city, my legs trying to carry me away.

"Calvin?"

I gulped air, climbing to consciousness. My back ached, as if I'd been kicked in the kidneys. No longer dreaming, I sat up on the couch in Frank Zerba's office. It took a few moments to get it straight, and a little longer to become aware of the woman sitting next to me. The smell drifted to me first, soap, and a fragrant sweat—Monica.

"Hey, it's OK. Calm down."

I fell against a large pillow. A blanket lay tangled at my feet. Slivers of dawn showed through the curtained window near the desk and bookcase. I had to quickly reconnoiter, and last night came back. Dezi had been beaten up pretty bad, but didn't want to go the hospital. We came back here and Zerba put her to bed. I talked to Manny, who apparently had been doing work on his end and he told me to stay in town, that a Detroit police detective wanted to talk to me in the morning.

I had also spoken to Monica who had not been happy to hear about our adventures. When she asked if I wanted her to come down, I had said not to worry. But she had. "Did you just get here?" I asked.

"A couple of hours ago."

We sat in silence. Now I caught a whiff of cigars in this room. Books filled shelves behind the desk. For a moment I thought of the meeting I had with the bishop in Grand Rapids and Barry Lazio. Then I recalled the strange dream. Brother Blanton, an evangelist who thrived on pitting his vision of hell against your vision of heaven. And the boy bleeding in the alley. "Have you checked Dezi?" I asked.

"She's sleeping, but her face looks awful." Monica wore a bulky sweater. Her blonde hair stuck up in curly bunches around her pale face. She looked tired and scared and mad. "What happened to her, Calvin?"

I told her, thinking of Oscar, his doughy chest and smirking mouth, which I had turned bloody. Then I felt sad, and a little ashamed. For some reason, that brought back the dream again. That youngster in the alley. My flight.

When I had finished, Monica slid closer and touched the sweat drying on my brow. Light grew at the window, casting a gentle hazy

125

glow on the couch and the side of Monica's face. Shuffling off the blanket at my feet, I touched her cheek, and she clasped my hand.

I imagined her driving down from Grand Rapids, fighting off sleep, wanting to be here. That made up for a lot. Thinking this, an undeniable pang shot through me, a feeling of an intense loneliness, or a recollection of it. The way I'd been feeling—that is, cut off and out there on the edge, and without knowing it—hit home and I nearly lost it. Instead, I sighed and pressed my forehead to hers.

But she pulled back, still close. "Why didn't you tell me you were coming down here with Bob?"

"That was a mistake."

"He could have been killed. And you, too, not to mention Dezi."

"I'm sorry."

Monica stiffened. Her expression held a mixture of anger and accusation and yet also of warmth and consideration.

"I wanted to help Manny," I tried to explain.

"You have church to take care of."

I sat up straight, aware that she was right. I served as a minister, not some half-cocked private detective. My job was to save souls, not solve crimes. And yet...

"Cal, you and who you want to help is one thing. But don't drag my brother into it."

I didn't feel up for a lecture. "A guy got killed trying to tell me something. Doesn't that count?"

"Of course, but I don't want you getting killed, too."

I opened my arms and she slumped into them. I held her tight for a minute or two, realizing how scared she felt. The trip down here in the middle of the night had to have been lousy.

"Look, I'm done with my part. I talk to the police and then head home."

She leaned back, brushing hair from her face. "Police?"

Someone tapped at the door. It opened a few inches, and Father Zerba poked his head in. He looked at us on the couch. "There's breakfast in the kitchen," he said. "I have to say Mass."

Zerba then pushed in a little farther, his body taking up much of the doorway. He wore a cardigan over his Roman collar. He peered at us, almost paternally. "A detective from the local precinct just called. Apparently he spoke to your friend, the captain, in Grand Rapids," the priest said. "He wants to talk to you about 10. Does that work?"

"It's fine."

"I'll drop you off, if you'd like, on my way to Dearborn."

Zerba shut the door, leaving us alone.

"Monica," I said, thinking I needed to explain myself in some essential way. "I should have told you we were coming here. But I had no idea what we'd run into."

"Calvin," she responded, "you know how Bob worships you. He'd follow you anywhere."

"I know."

I thought of telling her that Bob may be willing to follow me, but in this case other motivations were at work. Bob was daffy over Dezi.

"What do the police want?" she asked.

"I think to fill them in on last night."

The door opened again. But this time not so quietly. It flung our way, and her bear-sized brother appeared. "Speaking of the devil," I said.

Bob blinked, as if distracted, his fists at his sides, and then headed our way. Monica made room and he dropped between us.

Sleep had matted his hair. Wearing his Packers clothes, he smelled clean and fresh. "Blessed be the beekeepers," he said.

Monica smiled wanly and touched his hair.

"And all of us under heaven,'" Bob added, very pleased with being able to massacre scripture so early in the morning—first from the Sermon on the Mount and then Ecclesiastics.

His off-center Bible quoting made me realize I'd better get straight with God before doing anything else. I got up, telling Monica I was going to Mass.

Hues of light beamed through the stained-glass windows inside historic St. Anne's. The Catholics knew how to build churches. For a moment, I thought of the Cathedral of Saint Barnabas in Grand Rapids, and of the body they found. A young man who attacked his aunt and who had a tattoo of an Indian brave on his arm. Over a map? Also, I wondered, had he killed Melinda? They had had a fight, Mary Simon told Zerba.

I decided to stop thinking, at least for the time being, and drank in the architecture of the church.

The arched ceiling soared; the pillars stood firm and sturdy, etched in ancient, Roman script; the pews carried a glossy coloring of burgundy, and the altar served as a strong, marble anchor in the front. My mother had dragged me to Mass a few times in my youth, but mostly I went to the much more austere and certainly less ceremonial Christian Reformed service with my cranky but generally pious Hollander father.

Back then, as now, I felt a little weird around the centuries-old production of the Mass. The service held a stately otherworldly quality to it. But at the same time, and this is what bugged my Protestant sensibilities, it was a little too choreographed. It was easy to get lost in the ritual and to lose sight of the real deal, which was the man hanging from the cross on the far back wall above a bank of flickering, lightly smoking candles. Christ died for our sins, not to become the subject of a rote recitation of mostly man-made words.

But I wasn't here to debate theological sticking points. Along with Bob, and not with Monica, who went to tend to Dezi, I'd come to church to pray. I wanted to shake off the worldly torpor that had me in its jaws. I very much needed to put my head on right, and to link again with God, to break from the violence and blood. If not, I was better off finding another job. Because a minister shouldn't be a charlatan, preaching out of both sides of his mouth. He's only a tough guy in the service of God, and not out to promote his own cause. Giving Oscar the forearm bothered me, even though he deserved it. As for the Rogue Warrior with the club, he had had no idea that the priest knew how to throw a punch.

A gargled noise brought me back to the moment. Bob, kneeling on my left, had conked out and started snoring. Seeing that Zerba had gotten to the part where everyone was standing to say the Lord's Prayer, I nudged him in the ribs. His eyes popped open.

Bob blinked and rose along with the rest of us.

Holding Bob's hand and the hand of an elderly woman next to me, we prayed the "Lord's Prayer."

Next came the "Kiss of Peace," a folksy touch not mandated in our church. Instead of smooching, we shook hands with others in the row in front of us. I had to cut in on Bob since he had started pumping hands like he was running for office.

We'd just about finished kiss-of-peacing when I felt a poke in the shoulder. I turned to see a burly man with black hair, a mustache, penetrating eyes and a camel hair sport coat over a banana-colored turtleneck. Moments before I hadn't seen him in the pew, but now he was. Maybe he'd been beamed down from some dark planet. My hand froze as it reached out for his. "Peace, my friend," he said, grabbing and crushing my flesh.

I held on, watching him watch me. Something mean turned and stretched in Jamal's eyes; the mouth under the mustache curled. "Where's the fat whore?" he asked in a low voice.

People, I knew, watched us.

"She has a big mouth, and I need to talk to her."

Our eyes remained locked, until the congregation knelt. As Jamal dropped to his knees, I turned and did the same, fixed my attention on Zerba, who stood behind the altar, washed in a rainbow of light cascading through the windows.

The priest wore white robes; his scruffy hair looked like a burning bush and his weathered face was turned skyward. He raised the circle of bread in offering.

Soon, the faithful started sliding out of pews, filing up the aisle for communion.

Bob rose to let people slip by. Then praying hands under his chin, he followed. I thought of going after him. He wasn't Catholic, after

129

all. But I let him go, peering at the cross behind the altar and imagining what Christ endured to wash away our sins. I had to remember that. We were already forgiven.

Moments later, I turned around to see if Jamal remained in the pew. He was gone. He'd vanished. But his presence remained as a threat I couldn't ignore.

CHAPTER EIGHTEEN

The Detroit police detective, dressed in a tailored, double-breasted suit, green shirt and matching tie, scribbled notes on a legal pad. We were sitting at a big battered table in an unadorned room with green walls.

Before Zerba drove me over here maybe two hours ago now, I talked to Manny and he insisted that I be up front with this over-weight guy named Karl. Our appointment had been rescheduled for noon, but even then the guy was late. I had cooled my heels, reading through a stack of old Newsweeks and police union magazines in the hallway outside, before he showed. At one point, I used the pay phone to call my church for messages, and had a few. But one espe-cially, from the WMU history professor, grabbed my attention. He had left a nugget of information for me. Pieces were starting to fit.

Anyway, the Detroit cop and I had gone around and around for awhile, and it became clear he only wanted information from me, and wasn't going to give much in return. I was hoping he'd jump at the name of Jamal and offer to bring him in for questioning. Or, at the very least, ask more about Mohawk and the kidnapping. Or ask about Oscar and maybe tell me what he might know about the fat grocery store owner. But Karl just kept his lip buttoned on what all of this might mean and where it might lead and simply asked ques-tions about my purpose down here.

When we finally finished talking, or make that I finished telling him my story, Karl sat back, making his chair creak. He had a wide flushed face, watery eyes and sparse black hair combed sideways on his broad skull. "Tell me again where this hooker girl friend of yours is now?"

"You mean Dezi?"

He nodded.

"As far as I know, she's on the way back to Grand Rapids."

After Mass, I tried to talk to Monica, but she was on the phone, keeping up with church business, which of course I had been shirking. We finally spoke for a few minutes in late morning on the back porch looking out on the railroad building. It stood above everything else, showing off its ruined glory. I could see the floor, and even the window, where I'd been last night. The structure looked even more broken and dilapidated in the daylight.

I finally got around to telling Monica my concerns about Dezi, and tried to make amends for shutting her out and making this trip unannounced. I think I made a little headway on that account. As for Dezi, Monica said she would try to talk to her. The plan was to drive back to West Michigan, where Dezi could see a doctor if she felt the need. I was hoping to hit the road as soon as I was done here at the precinct house.

"Does Miss Dezi have a friend by the name of Russ Woods?" Karl then asked.

His question hit me out of the blue. He meant Wooly Bully. I told him about the tattoo parlor, then wondered why he asked.

The detective had come highly recommended from Manny. But I wasn't feeling good about the one-sided conversation.

"What about Russ Woods?" I asked.

Karl stared at me, his hands cupped over his notes, pretending to smile, and then leaned back in his seat. He shrugged. "Just wondering." Then the detective scratched an ear.

"What about Russ Woods?" I tried again.

Karl didn't answer.

"Look," I said, "I told you what I know."

"And I appreciate it. I certainly do."

"That's it?" I asked.

He shrugged.

I was steamed. All over the place I was getting guff and grief, and

I was sick of it. "So, what about Jamal and his friends?" I asked. "Are you going to bring them in? Or do they go free because they are such model citizens?"

He smiled, but he didn't mean it. "Sure, you bet. I'm going to type this report up, yes sir, and put it in my to-do pile. The one, you know, that has such things in it as a drunken father abusing his ten-year-old, a mother burning her kid's hands on the stove, a couple Homeboys robbing and torturing a gas station clerk."

"You're a busy man, detective."

He twined his fingers over his belly. "You bet I am. And when I file the report, I'm going get in my car and go get Mr. Jamal and his maggoty friends, bring them back here and put them through the ringer. And, I'll bet they will just outright unburden themselves to me. They'll tell me everything they can."

"They kidnapped us at a gun point."

He stared at me, sniffed and nodded, hands still crossed over his belly. "You did say that."

"And?"

He sat forward. "I'll talk to him, OK. But, from what you said, he wasn't the one who did the kidnapping. Jamal is no dummy."

"Is he big into the casino business?" I asked.

"Why?"

"I wonder if he might not like competition in Wayland."

"You going to have a regular little Las Vegas up there, are you?"

"You bet."

I don't think he got the pun, and so I decided to ask what he knew about Oscar.

He scowled. "Oscar is just one more piece of scum."

"That's helpful."

Karl smiled. "Look, Reverend, when we get something, if we get something, I'll call."

"Why did you ask about Russ Woods?"

Karl shrugged, running a hand down his tie and tucking it into place down the slope of his gut. "Word is he was down here, last night. He might have stopped over to that rooming house in Dearborn. The one where the lady in the hospital lives."

"You're kidding?"

The cop shook his head.

"How do you know this?" I asked.

Karl settled himself inside his suit, rubbed a hand over his hair, and sniffed the air again. "Oh, I heard it from the Dearborn cop who stopped him for speeding he might have broken into that apartment. He was looking for something." The Detroit detective looked a little punchy, as if he been up for days, and maybe he had.

"He's in jail?"

The detective leaned close, his breath fanning my cheek. "Actually, no. They let him go before we knew about the break-in. But the landlady described him pretty well."

"Did he find what he was looking for? Maybe a map of some kind?" I asked.

The detective smiled. "Like I said, stay by the phone." He reached into his coat, took out a card and slipped it across the desk. "You can also call me."

I took the card and stuck it in my pocket. "How did you get on to Russ Woods so fast, Detective, seeing as it happened in Dearborn?"

He pointed a finger at his head. "Go figure. There are other people who have my phone number, too."

Since Zerba had dropped me off and my truck was still back at St. Anne's, I walked the four blocks to the church. My legs felt heavy and I was still beleaguered by the dreams I'd had during the few hours of sleep I'd gotten on the couch. I was looking forward to being back in Wayland and trying to resume a normal routine. Yet, something nagged at me, a sense of failure. It seemed I'd learned a lot on the trip down here—a lot, but not what I'd truly come for.

Clouds had started to stalk the sky, casting ominous shadows over the railroad building, in front of which trucks now moved. A few were filled with debris, while others were pulling in. Zerba had said

134

the city continued to debate its fate, but Detroit officials had agreed to help with some cleanup of the depot. Again, I located where I'd met Jamal. He confounded me and I wondered how deeply involved he was in whatever it was that went down in Grand Rapids. I tried to put it together—a map, a fight between Melinda and Donny Johnson.

Walking through a small commercial district and into a neighborhood that sat near the foot of the Ambassador Bridge, I looked at the other pieces. The latest: Russ Woods. I stopped, trying to catch a fleeting thought. I felt too punchy to make sense of things.

Zerba wasn't there when I returned, and I didn't think he would be. He had said today, Thursday, was when he helped manage the food pantry at a small annex to St. Lazar's. I thought briefly of making a trip there to speak with him but decided against it. Instead, I knocked on the door to tell the secretary I was leaving and to ask Zerba to call me at home when he could.

She was the same woman I'd spoken with yesterday when I'd first wanted to talk to the priest. When she opened the door, she looked a little surprised, maybe even pleased, and yet worried. "Reverend Turkstra," she said. "You just had a call, and it sounded important."

She gave me the number and let me use the office phone. It was Dezi, talking to me on her cell.

"Reverend, don't you have your cell phone turned on" she said.

"The battery is dead. Where are you?"

"We're at the hospital. Something's happened to Monica."

My mind wasn't ready for this. Stupidly, I gazed at a framed photo of Pope John Paul II hanging from the wall by the doorway next to which the secretary now stood. A few years before, I made the trip down here with my mother when the pope held Mass at the nearby Silverdome. On the way back, we had driven by a bad accident. This is what I feared now.

But Dezi wasn't telling me about an accident. She said someone in a big white truck had abducted Monica from the parking lot of Detroit Receiving Hospital.

"What are you doing there?" I nearly shouted.

135

"She took me for stitches and to check my head. I nearly passed out in the car."

"But what happened to her?"

Dezi sounded very upset. "I don't know."

"Did you call the police?"

"Should I?"

"Wait until I get there."

I drove as quickly as I could to the hospital. When I arrived, I saw Dezi and Monica's brother pacing inside the emergency room.

Medics rolled people in on stretchers. People sat everywhere; some sprawled asleep on chairs. A few talked to themselves; a couple had bandages taped to their faces. Detroit Receiving was one of the bloodiest and busiest ERs in the state. A row of stitches rimmed the skin above Dezi's right eyelid.

"What happened?" I asked.

Dezi shook her head. "Monica went out for some air, but didn't come back."

A woman spun through one of the ER doors, flailing her arms, her hand swollen and red. A nurse rushed in from somewhere and took her away.

We went outside and stood in the shadow of the massive hospital. The parking lot stretched for a good two blocks. A slab of downtown showed out there. Bulky buildings; a web of expressways. A chilly wind had started to blow and gray clouds filled the sky.

Bob was wringing his hands.

"Go over it again," I said, trying to stay calm.

Dezi slammed a foot on the pavement. "I told you, she's gone. Maybe they took her, thinking she was me."

"Who would they be?"

"It doesn't matter."

"Like hell!" I yelled, unable to contain the curse.

She shrank back and Bob stepped to my side. He bumped my shoulder with his, wanting me to cool my jets.

I took a few breaths and asked, "Why would someone take Monica?"

"I gave her my coat, since it's cold out."

"Coat?"

"The one I was wearing, with all of the fringe."

I looked around, checking the lot, seeing the clouds in the sky, feeling the rush of mid-afternoon activity everywhere.

I turned back to Dezi. "You've been lying all along. Why should I believe you now?"

"I'm not lying."

"What about Wooly Bully? Why is he down here?"

Her bruised face sagged, her eyes were filled with tears, and her stitches looked tight and painful. Bob tried to comfort her, but she shrugged him away.

A stiff wind started, whipping in around us.

"Dezi, you set us up."

She shook her head, hugging her shoulders.

"Who would want to come after you?" I asked.

Dezi looked to the ground. Bob hovered near her; she elbowed him away. "We went to Oscar's," she said. "We drove by his store. I had to get my purse. Then, when we were leaving I started to get sick. I had to puke. And Monica brought me here."

"Are you crazy? You went by Oscar's?"

"I needed my purse."

I took a few breaths, scanning the parking lot for a white truck. My heart had turned into a fist. "When was this?" I asked.

"I told you, before coming here."

"Who would have taken her, Dezi?"

"Someone told a security guard it was man in a white truck with a white beard."

"Was there some kind of struggle?"

"I don't know."

"Where is the security guard now?"

"I don't know." Dezi looked sick, like she about ready to throw up again. She shook her head.

Wind raked itself against my face, telling me we were in for some bad weather. I felt weak and had to steady myself. I kept a lid on things by saying a very quick prayer—"Lord, don't let me kill her." I meant Dezi, and realized that my ministry was no longer a ministry. It was a chaotic tumble downhill. I was snared by dark emotions. "He thought she was you?" I asked.

Dezi nodded and grabbed her shoulders. "It had to be. I don't think this guy knows me." Dezi gazed at me with some hope on her face, or maybe it was pleading. "She had my coat. I should never have given it to her."

"Who is this guy?"

I don't know."

"Where did you guys park?" I asked, hoping against hope to find Monica there.

But her Corsica, parked along a far edge of the lot, was empty. I put my hand on the roof, bent and tried to think. Finally, I spun and faced Dezi. "Does this guy with the beard work for Oscar?"

"I don't know!"

"How about for Bully?"

Bob stood between us, trying to keep things from escalating. Air rushed out of my lungs, as if I'd been smashed in the back and gut at the same time.

Dezi's hair—her blonde dye job—was in tangles; dark circles hollowed her eyes. She infuriated me. Oscar had beaten her silly, and she had to go by for her purse. The magic purse. And Monica apparently went right along with it. But then that wasn't the worst of it by a long shot.

I knew we had to talk to Oscar.

But first I tried to find the security guard. When I couldn't find him, I called Karl, the detective. Fortunately, he was at his desk. When I told him what had happened, he told me to wait there. He would have a patrol car stop by to take a report.

"I'm giving you the report, now, over the phone!" I shouted, snapping off Dezi's cell and heading for my truck.

CHAPTER NINETEEN

Oscar's Grab 'n' Go didn't look very busy as I pulled into the lot. Only a couple cars were parked near the back. Paint peeled from the walls, beer banners flapped in the slight wind, garbage overflowed the can outside the front door.

"Do you want me to come in?" asked Dezi.

"I can handle it," I said.

On the way here, Dezi reluctantly explained some of what happened. She and Wooly Bully had been in this from the start. As far as I could tell, she hadn't talked to him yet.

I left her and Bob in the truck. Bleak apartment buildings lined the alley behind the party store. Barbed wire ringed the roof of the Grab 'n' Go. The wind still blew briskly, the clouds grew uglier.

The door to the store banged open when I pushed, a bell announcing my presence. A couple rows of snack food stood on my right; coolers filled to the gills with beer and pop were in back. Oscar stood inside a glass-enclosed area for the cashier. "What do you want?" he said, his voice muffled by the protective enclosure.

A program played on a small TV above Oscar; the figure on the screen moved just as I did. A video of me. "Where's Monica?"

Oscar rubbed a hand over his bald head. He licked at a blue bump at the corner of his mouth. He wore a flimsy tropical shirt over his paunch and white pants. A radio, tuned a to radio sports show, played.

"I don't know what you're talking about," he said, his muffled voice coming through a hole in the protective glass.

Anger welled in me, like water pushing a dike.

"So get out of here," he said.

Oscar then went on arranging packages of cigarettes on the counter.

"Did you know that it's not Dezi that they have?" I asked.

He stopped shuffling the cigarettes and then folded his hands over his gut as he sat on a tall stool. Watching me deadpan behind the glass, he rubbed a finger over his chin and then grabbed a mug on whose face was a Detroit Red Wings emblem. "Get lost."

I moved quickly, rounding the little booth. I tried the knob to the door. Locked. Oscar watched me now, very wary.

Then I turned, reared back and kicked the door.

It heaved, bent, and crashed open. I went after him.

He had pulled a handgun out of a drawer, and he used it to back me off. I froze, sickened to be this close to him. The tiny room stank of stale food and sweat. Of course, smashing in his door could be construed as reason enough to shoot me. I wasn't sure if he was up to it, but he looked close to deciding.

"Where is she?" I demanded.

He stuck the gun in my gut.

"Oscar, leave him alone."

It was Dezi, come to the rescue. "What bullshit were you telling him?" he asked.

Dezi squeezed next to me. I thought I heard customers in the store, but didn't dare look. "Who took Monica?" she asked, pointing her own gun, the one from her purse, at him. I had forgotten all about it. Or, rather, the one she took out at some point and stuffed beneath the seat of my truck. She had told me that.

Oscar's teeth looked brown. His eyes were shifty. "Who's Monica?" He breathed hard. His shirt, showing palm leaves and dancing natives, swelled at the belly, the buttons about to break. A circle of sweat had spread under his arms. I backed a few inches from his gun.

I stayed as still as I could, but then I heard something crash against the security window. Oscar pivoted that way.

I took this chance to act, clamping an arm around his neck and hammer-locking him against the counter. Out of the corner of my eye, I saw Bob picking up display cases and whipping them at the window. They crashed and broke against the partition. Bags of pretzels and corn chips went flying.

Oscar's lips twisted as he lay on one side of his face. The gun had dropped to the floor. I kicked it aside, toward Dezi who bent and picked it up. Now she had two. "Tell me. Where is she?"

He burbled a response, spit spewing. Meanwhile Bob stuck his lips flat against the window, making like a fish. "Where?'"

Dezi nudged her gun barrel into one of Oscar's ears. He strained to see what she was up to. Calm concentration masked her face, her lips thin, and her arm steady.

Bob wedged into the room, shoving Dezi closer and jamming the metal deeper into Oscar's ear. Packed tight, I had to let up a little on him. "Who is the guy with the white beard?" I asked.

Hearing more commotion in the store, I glanced over and saw a couple teens standing inside the door, arms swinging. One of them was Alonzo, the black kid from last night. He now wore a canary-colored sweatshirt and lime green pants. A fuzzy cap sat on his head. His eyes got big when he saw the scenario. A couple of guns, me, Oscar still sprawled on the counter. Dezi. Bob.

I squeezed out, facing the teens. They looked excited and a little wary. My shoes crunched bags of chips.

"Who works for him?" I asked, swinging an arm at Oscar. "Does he have a man who drives a white truck – a guy with a white beard?"

Bob joined me, causing the kid and his partners to slide back, as if they'd come to the lip of a bubbling volcano.

Alonzo's body seemed to vibrate. I saw a glint of greed, the notion that there was likely something in this for him, as there had been last night, flicker across his face. Aware of what would make him helpful, I dug out my wallet, opened it and slipped out two twenties.

The kid nodded for his partners to back off, maybe to man the door, as if to keep anyone else out while he conducted business. Alonzo gazed at the grocer.

Dezi's chest heaved, her hand still hovered, fingers wrapped around the trigger. She had put away the other gun apparently.

Tattoos showed on her shoulders, a bleeding of ink that matched the color of the bruises on her battered face. I was thinking I ought to get the guns from her.

Bob toed a package of Ho Hos. He bent, picked them up, but didn't open them.

Alonzo tilted his head, maybe to get a better look at me. Then he checked out Oscar again.

I fingered out another 20, the last of my bankroll.

Again, his eyes shifted to Oscar.

Oscar cursed and called the kid a racist name. But Dezi was right there, ordering him to shut his trap.

"Hey, man," the kid said, pointing at Oscar. "If I don't tell them, she's gonna waste you."

The grocer was still, looking like a trapped animal, a weasel, maybe.

Alonzo stared at the bills in my hand, then his eyes slid to Bob.

"Who are we talking about?" he asked.

"A guy in a big pickup who has a white beard."

Alonzo scowled at the money, maybe wondering was it worth it to be a stool pigeon. I guess it was. "Right, some dude with a beard. That's all I know. Left awhile ago, but I don't know nothing about no kidnapping or like that."

"He was here?"

"Yeah."

"Do you know him?"

"Never saw him before."

"Was he alone?"

"I think so."

"Does he work for Oscar ?"

Alonzo gazed at Oscar behind the glass. "Naw. Two of them were, like, arguing."

"About what?"

"I guess her." Alonzo pointed at Dezi, still with her gun trained on Oscar.

Questions swirled, and time was slipping away. If I wanted to find Monica, I needed to make much better headway than this.

"Tell me, this, Alonzo, do you know a man named Jamal?"

"Everyone knows him."

"Does Oscar work for him?"

"Lots of people work for Jamal."

"How about the guy in the white truck?"

Oscar yelled for him to shut up.

"Does he?" I demanded.

"Man, like I told you, lots of people work for that Arab."

"How about him?"

"Could be, but I don't know."

Maybe I was reaching for straws, but I took that to mean yes.

An hour later, Mohawk hauled open the metal doors and gave me the evil eye. Then without as much as a long-time-no-see, he turned and started up a winding narrow staircase.

Father Zerba and I followed his black leather coat as it swept around several bends. We took the back way into a building not far from Zerba's church that housed a Lebanese restaurant and the office out of which Jamal conducted business.

I had called the priest, explained what had happened, and he said to come right over. By the time we appeared at his rectory, he had done some work and set up this meeting with Jamal. I had also called Manny, who told me that confronting Jamal on our own was suicide. He told me to call Karl, to back off, and let the experts take over. I asked him to call Karl.

Two flights up, we came to a small landing. Mohawk knocked on a door, twisted the knob and squeezed against the wall to let us in. I bumped against something hard as I slipped by him. A weapon inside that coat. The only weapon I had—actually, it was Dezi's—was back under the seat in my truck, which I had parked outside, leaving Bob and Dezi to listen to oldies on the radio. We had dumped Oscar's gun in the trash outside of his store. We left him inside, shaken but unhurt.

143

Zerba went first and I followed into a spacious room. A row of large windows on the right overlooked Vernor Avenue.

A huge aerial photograph showed hundreds of thousands of people gathered around a small building. It looked like the pilgrimage to Mecca.

The photo hung behind a desk, beyond which Jamal, wearing a white suit and black shirt, now stood.

"Father Zerba, welcome."

Jamal had penetrating eyes, the color of hot asphalt, hair curling on the collar of the shirt and a thin mouth under the bushy mustache.

We approached his desk slowly, and he watched us come, hands folded. His eyes seemed to burn through me. I noticed crossed swords in a corner by another door and the statue of a panther, about the size of a fire hydrant, on one side of the shiny, expansive marble-topped desk. But my eyes ran back to that large photo.

"Thank you for seeing us on such short notice, Mr. Jamal," said the priest, stopping at the edge of a beige carpet, rimmed in roses, arranged under the desk.

Mohawk had sidled over to the door by the swords.

Jamal opened and closed those hands, which looked surprisingly prissy and petite. Those eyes touched on the priest, then back to me. "The cardinal can be very persuasive," he said to me.

I turned to Zerba, who looked a little embarrassed. He briefly explained that one of the priests living at St. Anne's was a retired bishop, who, it turns out once worked for Cardinal Anslem Smith, leader of the local archdiocese. The bishop had called his former boss, who apparently dialed Jamal and here we were.

"The cardinal is a friend," Jamal explained.

"Did the cardinal ask you to help me?" I asked.

A quick smile twisted one corner of his mouth. "Would either of you like a drink?" He gestured at amber-colored liquid inside a decanter on his desk.

I now edged onto the carpet. Only a few feet separated me from Jamal. I wondered if this man was a practicing Muslim, or Christian, or neither, or in some fashion both. Devout Muslims neither drank nor smoked. I wasn't sure if they gambled or owned casinos. But his religious affiliation didn't matter right now. "Can you help me or not?" I demanded.

His expression hardened. "Father, is he going to make trouble? I'm only doing this as a favor. I have a very busy schedule."

Zerba didn't respond, just stood there, his large hands cupped at his sides, a wheeze sounding in his nose.

"You're not standing in the office of my restaurant to cause me any problems, are you, my friend?" Jamal asked me.

"You bet I am."

He wasn't sure what to make of that. "I thought we had agreed last night that you would go back to Grand Rapids."

"That's before someone kidnapped my girlfriend. If I don't get her back and fast, I'm going to the police."

"That would be wise. It's their job to handle a kidnapping."

"But that's not all I'm going to talk to them about."

"And what, my friend, does that mean?"

"You add it up."

Mohawk shifted at his perch and adjusted something inside that coat. His face was long and tan and profoundly serene.

I felt Zerba's hand on my arm, warning me to cool it.

Jamal looked at the priest, as if asking was the tall minister he'd brought along out of his gourd.

The priest began to talk, explaining what I feared happened to Monica.

"Why come to me?" Jamal asked.

"Oscar," I said, putting that slab of flab right into the pressure cooker, where he belonged. I was well aware of thin ice I was treading. I could almost hear it crack and start to give. But what other choice did I have? So I did some speculating. "He's the one who ordered the kidnap," I said.

Jamal made a quick move with his head, motioning at his bodyguard. Mohawk took it in, apparently catching an unspoken request, opened the door and left.

Jamal then gestured in the direction of the windows. Three leather armchairs faced the glass. "Please, sit."

Zerba caught my eye, indicating to follow directions, and so we plopped in seats that sighed as we settled in. Jamal brought a lit cigar and drink, wedged his chair to face us, and then sat. He held the glass to his nose, smoke fogging the air between us. I decided if he was a follower of Islam, that he was fallen away. If he was Christian, I'm not so sure we revered the same Christ. "Reverend," he said. "What are you saying about Oscar Nassan?"

"You do know him?"

"Of course."

I was anxious to move this forward, but also knew I needed to be careful. He sipped his drink, delicately took in smoke, and crossed his legs. He was crafty and probably just as powerful as I'd been led to think. "So, what do you want?" he asked.

"Call Oscar and find out where she is. I want her back, and I need your help, Mr. Jamal," I finally answered.

"What makes you think I have anything to do with this?"

"My sense is not much happens around here without you knowing."

His eyes clicked, calculating, a small smile on his mouth. "What are you saying about Oscar?"

Zerba had been very still. But he now leaned forward in his seat. Traffic flowed below. Music played somewhere, maybe in the restaurant beneath us. "He wanted to grab the one called Dezi, but got this man's girlfriend instead."

Jamal smoked and stared at me. He emanated the same chilly scrutiny I'd felt in the railroad building. His eyes swam with a kind of reptilian intelligence as he addressed me. "What does Oscar want with the whore?" he asked.

"What do you want with her?" I cut in, referring to his appearance at church.

Jamal's eyes smoldered. "Where is the whore now?"

I turned to Zerba, asking for help. "We don't know," he answered.

Jamal set the liquor on a small table next to him. Poked out his skinny cigar in an ashtray next to the half-full glass. "Father, where is the whore?"

Zerba kept calm; he didn't flinch. "I'm not sure."

Jamal's expression shifted, only slightly, to calculation. "No man in a white truck works for me."

"Who does he work for then?"

We waited. When he didn't answer, I asked, "Mr. Jamal are you involved in trying to keep a gambling casino out of Wayland? Would it cut into your business down here?"

Animal fury leapt into Jamal's eyes. I'd hit a hot spot. But then he smiled. "My friend, I don't have any idea what you mean."

"Which means you know where Monica is?"

Jamal set the glass on the table and dropped his smoldering cigar into a half-inch of liquid. "I told you. No man in a white truck works for me."

I climbed half out of my seat. "Who does he work for?"

Jamal sat back, gazing at me. Our eyes locked. I waited. We were in some very deep and dangerous water. Finally, Jamal spoke: "I don't know anything about this. I can talk to Oscar, but I'm sure he won't either."

I wanted to ring his neck. But Zerba touched my knee. "Then we're sorry for taking up your time, Mr. Jamal," said the priest.

I wanted to protest big time. But something in the priest's expression held a warning and a promise.

We all got up at the same time.

My gaze fell a moment on that scene of so many people gathered around a holy shrine. People drawn together by their deep faith to pray.

"Mr. Jamal," I said, "is that Mecca?"

He didn't look at the enlarged photo. Instead he remained fixed on me. "We're finished here tonight."

"My religion asks us to help others when we can, especially when their lives are in danger," I said. "What about yours? My sense is that Islam teaches a lot about reaching out. I believe your prophet

147

preached peace."

Rage coursed through Jamal. I saw it in his face and in his hunched stance. "You know nothing about Islam," he said softly. "Get out."

Going on half an hour later, I stood next to my truck, listening vaguely to a mixture of music. Tim McGraw, crooning a love song to his lady love, Faith Hill, coming from the front seat of my Ford, in which Bob pretended to drive while Dezi dully slouched against the door on her side. From the restaurant floated Middle Eastern music, a sound of strings and horns.

The sky was nearly dark, even though it hadn't reached eight o'clock. Clouds continued to gather and the temperature had dropped. My mood, however, fell even faster. I was hopeless and scared.

Cars whizzed by on Vernor. Lights from nearby businesses bled into the night, creating a soft haze. The air smelled dense, a little like ozone, like a power gathering strength.

Dezi now got out of the car. Bob glanced at her without pausing, still steering, his mouth making motor sounds.

"When's the priest coming back?" Dezi asked.

"Soon."

Once we had reached the exit, Zerba told me to go ahead, and he then returned up the stairs to Jamal's office. I assumed he was going to make another plea with me out of hearing range. I wondered, though, what was taking him so long.

Given Jamal's interest in Dezi, I had wondered if he had sent Mohawk out to find her. I was sort of hoping she would be gone when we got out of there.

Dezi sniffed the air, then laid her arms on the roof on my Ranger. She peered at me. "This is my fault." Her eyes shone, catching light from the sky.

As a minister, it was my job to model forgiveness. But I didn't feel it now. So I didn't even try to pretend. I left her alone with her guilt.

148

"I tried to call Wooly while you were in there," she said. "But his girlfriend told me she hasn't heard from him yet."

"Where is he?"

"I don't know."

I wondered if she was telling the truth.

"Dezi," I said, "did Wooly Bully find this map or not?"

"I don't know!"

She stood straight. Bob's arms worked the steering wheel. Maybe in his mind he was hot on the track of finding Monica. The way things were going, he was probably doing a better job of it than me.

Dezi's face, in the pale light of the parking lot, looked misshapen. Although she had led to Monica's situation, she had paid a price. I hated to think what might have happened to her if we hadn't showed last night. A variety of conflicting interests, most of them outside the bounds of the law, were at play here. And I knew we were caught in the volatile cross-section of them.

"Reverend," Dezi said.

I let her go on.

"The thing is, Oscar wasn't in on this, not this time. I'm sure of it. I heard him talking. And that's why he was so pissed—someone else was putting it over on him."

"Putting what over?"

"It has to do with this map."

"Who are you talking about?"

"Maybe this guy with the white beard. I just know that Oscar has some really crappy people working for him. And none of them are below screwing him or anyone else royal if they get the chance." Her eyes were watery, her arms again resting on the roof of my truck. "Yours truly having been one of them."

I appreciated and warmed to her honesty. "So, Oscar set up this kidnapping to get you for what reason?"

She didn't answer for several seconds. "I told you. He didn't set it up."

"How did you even know about a map?"

149

"I heard him talking last night."

"And he thinks, what, that you and Wooly Bully have it?"

"Maybe he does now."

Great, I thought. She switched jackets with Monica and essentially signed her death warrant.

"Dezi, do you know what this map is to?"

"I think it's more than a map, and that the kid who died in the cathedral had buried it."

"Where? Why?"

"I don't know!"

"How do you know this?"

"From Wooly Bully."

"How does he know?"

"He talked with someone."

"Who?"

"I don't know."

Zerba appeared. He paused a second, checked the parking lot, and then hustled our way.

His blew on his hands as he stopped next to Dezi. "Park your truck down the street, Reverend. I'll pick you up in mine. But let's hurry."

"Where're we going?"

"We're going to follow that truck." He pointed to a vehicle parked along the side, near the front of the restaurant. I hadn't noticed it before. It was the Hummer. It looked like the same one in which Bob and I rode in last night.

"Where is it going?" I asked.

"I'll tell you on the way."

So I climbed in, nudging Bob over, and noticed Zerba and Dezi talking out there. She opened the door and told me she was going with him.

The radio rocked out a twangy tune about some woman's luck with the lottery as I backed out and wheeled onto the residential street that took me to a four-cornered stop sign. Seconds later, the priest's Tracker appeared in my mirror.

Bob switched off the radio and looked at me.

It was happening fast. I reached under the seat and grabbed Dezi's gun, locked the Ranger and took the front seat Dezi had just vacated so she could sit in the back with Bob.

Zerba eased down the block, making a U-turn just before we got to the restaurant. He parked at the curb.

Seconds later, the Hummer pulled out of the lot, drifting the other way. I think Mohawk drove. He was alone.

Zerba waited for the Hummer to reach the end of the block, where it turned left. "Say your prayers, Reverend."

"Where is he going, Father?"

"Where we might be able to find Reverend Smit."

"So Oscar is in on this?"

"I don't think so."

We rode north to Livernois, rolling by row upon row of businesses that displayed Arabic script on the front. People were out in droves. It was like another world.

Then we hit the Detroit limits, entered a rundown industrial district and headed east for a mile or so. The Hummer's lights seemed to float in front of us, drawing us on. "Where exactly is he going, Father?" I asked.

The priest looked alert and easy, his hands loose around the wheel. As the Hummer turned onto the ramp leading south on I-75, Zerba slowed, downshifting and checking me. "Trust me here."

We entered the expressway and shot into the left lane, joining the flow of traffic. The Hummer buzzed along, on the other side of a step-van.

"We need to call the police," I said.

But Zerba didn't answer.

Neighborhoods started to give way to the outskirts of the massive Ford Rouge Assembly Plant.

I edged as far up in my seat as I could get, watching the Hummer roll down the freeway, still within our grasp.

We were silent for quarter mile or so. "Father, did you talk to Jamal?"

Zerba was motionless behind the wheel, as if holding his breath. "Father, talk to me?'" I wondered.

"I spoke to the cardinal again. He called in a very big favor. Then he and Jamal talked."

"What…" He held up a hand, quieting me. "You had told me about the interest up in Grand Rapids in the diocese. He spoke to someone up there."

"Who?"

"I think the chancellor." He meant Nash.

"What did he learn?"

"I hope we'll find out soon."

The Tracker rocked a little as the odometer stayed steady at 75 mph. "Reverend, does Monica have this map or whatever it is?" asked the priest.

"You've got to be kidding me!"

The Hummer swept along a curve, moving away from the sprawling Ford factory, headed east now.

Zerba crossed lanes, shot around a motorcyclist, and then aimed for the far right lane. "Dezi?" I said, turning around. "Call Wooly's girlfriend again and ask where he is."

"Do you have any idea how pissed he's going be at me?" Her bruised face made her look like an oversized rag doll. Bob held her hand.

I decided not to push it, watching as she gazed beyond me, as if trying to decide finally where her allegiances lay. Apparently, she concluded to keep quiet.

Zerba suddenly swung back into the center lane. I realized we had lost the Hummer. I pounded the dash in frustration. Black smoke from three semis spewed in front of us. But then I saw a quick flash of the military-looking SUV dart off onto the entrance to the Southfield freeway.

The priest punched it, bounced us onto the shoulder, his hands on the wheel. "Sit tight, children."

Zerba cut off a truck, wrenched the wheel hard right, and flew in front of a rusty Pontiac that nearly lost it and crashed into the concave median strip. Horns blasted; lights flashed, and the road seemed to blur, but somehow the priest got us onto the other freeway.

Zerba had to weave in and out of traffic to catch up. By the time he did, the Hummer had shot up the exit to Grand River Avenue.

Traffic passed in the intersection at the top of the ramp. Ugly, bent-over trees stood to the right; a huge steeple-topped Pentecostal church rose beyond them. Bob smacked my shoulder, grunted and started pointing.

"There," I said, catching the direction Bob showed. "Left!"

Zerba jumped into traffic, bouncing on rutted, uneven pavement veering away from a swerving car, and headed for them. He turned to me. "Have you said that prayer yet, Reverend?" he asked.

CHAPTER TWENTY

Zerba blew the red light, zigzagging around traffic, and started down Fenkell, a rough road in need of major repair. We rode through Brightmoor in far northwest Detroit, closing in on the suburbs. Taillights flashed up ahead as the Hummer careened onto a side street.

A tall fence, topped by knots of bent steel, surrounded what looked like a former gas station. A handful of teens in long coats watched us make the turn. Maybe a block in front of us, the Hummer hung a left.

Rows of sagging homes—gutted hulks, ugly eyesores—ran on both sides of the street. We zipped by an empty lot, about two blocks behind the Hummer. "He's stopping," said Zerba.

The Hummer pulled into a driveway of a small house—a broken-down shell of a place. Bars covered the windows. "Where are we?" I asked.

"Jamal sent his man here and told me I could follow."

"Jamal?"

"Believe it or not, Reverend."

"The cardinal told him to go here?"

Zerba didn't answer. He was still a couple houses away when Mohawk hopped out of the Hummer. Moving fast and dipping low, he ran up the driveway toward what I took to be a side porch.

We pulled to a stop in front.

"That looks like a drug house," said Dezi.

As I started to crack open the door, bright light filled the air, suffusing the front yard with an unearthly glare. I heard several quick pops and then an explosion. More light and then flames blasted from the house. Sound reverberated through the air.

I got out and started to run for the house. But my foot caught on something and I fell to the ground. Waves of heat pummeled my face.

"Bob, get back here!" I heard behind me.

Monica's brother raced for the home, making for the shooting pillars of fire. I climbed up and went after him, seeing flames race from the basement. Another explosion, this one not as loud or intense, blew out the front windows. Glass flew at me, sending me to my knees. I couldn't see. Someone ran past me.

I got up, shielding my face from the blast-furnace heat.

Bob and Dezi emerged from the driveway side of the home, her arm around him, yanking him our way. She had captured him before he could get inside. His face was blackened. Flames flashed out, shoving them forward and to the ground.

I got up, knowing I had to get closer.

"Reverend," said Zerba, appearing next to me. "There are a couple people running from around back. One's a woman that looks like Monica."

Huge red shadows danced everywhere. "Where?" I asked.

The priest gestured. "Other side, heading for that side street. There's a white Silverado parked there."

"Take care of them," I told Zerba, meaning Bob and Dezi. Then I made for the street. Heat chased me as I ran.

Rounding the side of a house, I saw what looked like a large 4-by-4 pickup, resting on huge wheels, parked next to an alley that ran behind the burning house.

I saw two people—both small, the first hunched and light-haired, wearing a long coat with frills. It had to be Monica. The one behind was a man.

"Hey!" I called, reaching in my waistband for Dezi's gun.

The man shoved Monica in the passenger's side, slammed the door and rounded the front. "Stop!" I screamed.

He didn't hear, or if he had, he ignored my command.

Fifteen feet separated me from the truck when it jerked and bounced from the curb. I heard the engine roar and saw a pair of Tasmanian devils staring at me from the oddly illuminated mud flaps.

Shoving the gun back into my pants, I headed straight for the devils. Luckily, the truck got hung up for a couple seconds, the back wheels catching and spinning up dirt, trying to grab hold.

I leapt up and between the devils. My arms came to rest on the lip of the tailgate, and my legs whipped from under me as the Silverado got a grip and screeched away. I dangled, the momentum slamming my feet against the far side of the truck, but they came to rest on the thick rubber running board.

The truck slowed for a couple seconds, maybe for an intersection. As it did, I shoved myself up and over. Inertia carried me into the truck bed. My elbows smashed the metal floor and my head knocked against a wheel well. The rest of my body slammed into something that wasn't hard, but it wasn't real soft either.

Rolling over and lying there, I noticed stars shooting overhead. But those were my own stars, which I had to blink away. Then I saw the branches of trees whipping by, and the flash of streetlights. The Chevy flew. My head throbbed. As best I could tell, the driver was paying me no mind.

He kept on trucking. The knobby tires pounded the pavement and heavy-duty shocks cushioned the ride. The driver, I was pretty sure, had a white beard. My ears rang, and my head ached. I heard sirens and what sounded like thunder in the distance.

Wind rushed around me. I scooted around and tried to see into the small square windows in the back of the pickup's cab. But they were dark.

Bags filled with rattling cans lined one side of the truck bed. Pushed up against them were what I took to rolled blankets. On the other side was what looked like a large athletic bag and maybe a ladder.

Bouncing with the motion of the 4-by-4, I slid to my knees, trying to keep low, and looked behind me. We rode down a street lined with mostly closed businesses. A few cars drove behind us. To the left, I saw a rising plume of smoke.

I suddenly rocked backward and went sprawling as the Chevy came to an abrupt stop. This time I rolled and my legs swept across those blankets and slammed into the paper bags. Bottles and cans flew out, making a tremendous racket. When the noise finally ceased, the truck shot forward again, forcing my body to slide toward the middle.

Inside the cab a light came on, a soft orange glow appeared behind the square windows. I saw the outline of a face pressed against one of the windows. Then I heard the window slide open. "Is that you, Calvin?"

"Monica?"

I shoved up, crushing a couple cans with my elbows, and scooted her way.

A backwash of air blasted my face as I tried to talk through that porthole. Keeping my balance wasn't easy.

"Are you OK?" I asked.

"Where's Bob?"

"Still back at that house."

She sat on the small shelf seat behind the driver. I could see his face better, lit by the green light from the dash. He had a white beard.

"You better sit your butt down, buddy, until I get on the freeway," he shouted over his shoulder.

"Who are you?" I yelled back. But then he swung onto the road, which sent me sprawling. My head thudded into cans.

To top it off, I heard more thunder, saw a shaft of lightning fork across the sky and then felt cold needles cut into my face and pepper the back of my neck. It began raining hard. Sheets of driving water hit me, splashing everywhere. I held a hand over my eyes, trying to see Monica. A semi truck thundered by, churning up a backwash. Rivulets ran down my back.

"Shut the window!" the guy demanded.

I thought of grabbing for my gun and ordering him to pull over.

But Monica slid the window shut, leaving me to deal with the downpour. I looked around, seeking shelter and spotted a folded tarp

157

by the ladder. As I bent down and grabbed it, I felt a weight inside. Unfolding, the material, I came across a full six-pack of beer. I threw it aside and climbed under the tarp.

Questions nagged me as water beat on the tarp. I could try to get the drop on White Beard, but decided to wait until he stopped.

In fact, I tried to clear my head, aware I'd be called into action soon enough. I needed to conserve my energy and come up with a plan. But any plan, I knew, depended on what happened next. I was happy, though, to know Monica was safe.

Then an image hit me. We had been on the freeway and came to a stop outside of Lansing two days before when a white pickup with Tasmanian devils shot by. The driver had looked our way. White Beard had been following us and nearly rear-ended my Ranger. I don't recall having seen him tail me. I scoured my memory, trying to recall if he had been alone in the truck. I think he had.

Probably it was the noise, or possibly the pickup gaining speed and criss-crossing lanes that brought me back. White Beard was trying to elude someone. The tarp was a little tricky to throw aside.

Once I had it off, I saw headlights blazing less than 10 feet from the back of the 4-by-4. Someone was chasing us in a van.

The Silverado rocked and jerked, and I nearly lost my balance, as White Beard put the Chevy into high gear.

We were still on a freeway. The rain had slowed and wisps of fog started to form. I felt the power of the 4-by-4 under me, eating up pavement. But the van kept pace with us.

Running parallel, the van veered close, the passenger's window slid down and Mohawk appeared, holding a small semi-automatic rifle. I had thought he had been caught in the fire. Arnold was driving.

Since I was staying low, I don't think they saw me.

Then the van suddenly swerved into us. Metal met metal.

We raced next to one another for a few seconds before the van tried it again. This time White Beard braked and swung right. The van came along with him. But now Mohawk was even with me.

Half out of the window, he was trying to take aim at White Beard's window. I still didn't think he could see me. I grabbed for my gun, but it was wet and slipped out of my hand. I swept the floor with my hands, trying to grab it, but instead found two full cans of beer—one for each of my hands. These would have to do. Getting a good grip and balancing on my knees, I swung back, took aim and let go with the right.

The can crashed against the door just under Mohawk. Now he spotted me and turned the weapon my way. I'd already let the other go with my left. This time I hit his shoulder.

By the time he began to shoot, I'd dived for the floor.

Very carefully, I looked up after maybe a minute. Fog billowed between us, and they were lost, but not for long. The van quickly emerged from the soup, maybe a dozen feet behind us.

It was gaining, its headlights glaring. I knew Mohawk was going to rip on me first this time.

I quickly searched the truck bed, spotted the gun, but had a better idea. Instead of shooting bullets into the fog, I grabbed that ladder. It was aluminum and fairly light, but sturdy enough to cause trouble. The wind made it hard for me to grab and get it properly positioned to throw. The thing tilted and tottered, almost causing me to lose it. But I held on and hauled it over my read, squinting against the headlights, praying Mohawk didn't shoot me.

The van slowed and plowed through the fog into the other lane.

That was better. I swung left and flung the ladder into the road, where it bounced once and then rammed the front of the van. I heard a terrible clatter and crunching. Bulls-eye!

Then I fell to my knees. This time when I looked back, they were gone, lost in the clouds of fog.

CHAPTER TWENTY-ONE

White Beard finally pulled off onto a side road and parked by a ditch next to a cornfield. My body felt pretty beat up as I jumped over the side onto the road on Monica's side of the Chevy.

Her door flung open. But she sat there, looking at me. She didn't appear hurt. I offered my hands, which she took and then climbed out. I wrapped her in my arms. She felt soft and warm and her body trembled. My body shook, too.

White Beard meanwhile looped an arm over the steering wheel and turned to me, the light from inside showing a small square face, hair brushed back on his forehead and a close-cropped, Hemingway-style growth. He gave me an angry look, but didn't say anything.

"Did he hurt you?" I asked.

She shook her head and collapsed against me. I had to brace myself to hold her up. Monica started crying, but she got hold of herself pretty quickly and pulled back. "Did you throw something at that van?"

I nodded. "Who is he?" I asked, indicating White Beard who had climbed out on his side of the truck.

"I think his name is Parker."

I felt terrible for involving her like this, and wanted to tell her so. I also wanted to reassure her that the worst was now over. But I didn't know that for sure.

"Where's my beer?" Parker had climbed into the truck bed.

"Some of it's still there," I said.

"What about my ladder?"

"The ladder saved our lives."

It was probably about 10 p.m. The night was chilly and wet. Wisps of fog were lifting off a field of dying cornstalks; a full moon had risen out there, appearing behind marching clouds.

Monica broke completely away, wiping something from her face. She was so small, her hair a mess, the night shimmering in her eyes, that coat draped around her. Her face looked pained and very pale.

"Is Bob OK?"

"I think so. I left him with Dezi and the priest."

Parker popped the top of a can and swore. I think he got foamed.

"Did he kidnap you?" I asked.

"He was one of them."

"Who was the other?"

"Some idiot with lots of tattoos came along later. I think Dezi works for him."

It had to be Wooly Bully. The picture started to clear. "When he saw me, he knew they made a mistake," she said.

"Where is he now?"

"I have no idea."

"Was he in that house?"

"He left before it exploded. I think they make drugs there."

"Made."

Monica nodded, wiping a hand over her mouth. I saw her sway a bit. She looked dazed. She took in a deep breath or two. "I'll be right back," she said after moment, nodding at woods behind us. But before she left, I grabbed her hands.

"I'm glad you're safe."

Her eyes searched mine. "Parker thought I was Dezi," she said.

"I know."

Then she left, disappearing into the trees.

"Hey," I heard from the other side of the truck. "Where's she going?"

My knees hurt as I walked around to where he stood, beer in hand. A small, bow-legged man, Parker wore a jean jacket and black pants. No streetlights lit this deserted road. But the sky was clearing fast and the moon cast down enough of glow for me to see him pretty clearly.

"Who do you work for, Mr. Parker?"

161

He looked beyond me. The air carried a hint of skunk and manure. Maybe, I thought it emanated from him. Not far away, I heard Monica getting sick. He heard her, too. I saw his eyes slide her way. This guy was to blame, but then so was I.

Silence settled between us, two men facing one another, neither sure of the other.

"Who do you work for?" I demanded, finally taking out the gun.

He checked it out and wiped a hand over his beard. "I don't know what you're talking about."

"You're a liar," I said.

I heard Monica gagging and coughing and gagging some more.

"Who do you work for?"

He didn't answer.

"Where's Wooly Bully?"

Recognition shone on his face.

"Was he back at that drug house?"

Parker didn't answer.

"Were you two working together?"

"I don't know what you're saying."

"You were following me the other day, weren't you?"

"Screw off."

"Does Wooly Bully have a map?"

Parker spit on the ground as an answer.

I stuck the gun close to his chin. "Talk to me, Parker."

"Wooly Bully is an asshole."

"Does he have the map?"

Parker's eyes had grown wide. "I don't know. I ran into him in Detroit. I never met him before."

"Down where—in that woman's apartment?"

"Something like that."

Hearing more gagging and coughing, I said, "Stay where you are." I kept him in my sights while I reached in the cab of his truck, found and pocketed his keys. I figured I'd force him to drive us to Grand Rapids, where Manny could talk to this guy.

Around the other side of the truck, the cornfield opened up, washed in the milky luster of the moon. Stubby cornstalks bent over, as if trying to hide from the light. In the distance, traffic rushed and I spotted a smudge of city lights. We were probably 10 miles northwest of Lansing, just outside the small town of Portland. To the left, starkly etched against a dark wall of trees stood a barn and farmhouse. I thought of Psalm 19, "The heavens declare the glory of God." But that glory was a very mixed bag right now. "Monica?"

Getting no answer, I started into a small stand of scrubby woods. Leaves rustled underfoot, and the silver streams of light fell between the outstretched gnarly branches I had to shove out of the way as I trudged.

I called her name again.

"Over here."

I stepped around two twisted bushes and reached the edge of the rolling field. She knelt, face upturned, as if trying to catch some of that light from the moon. She was slender, shoulders rounded, her short hair touched here and there with a glossy shimmer. I could smell her sickness. Even so, she made me think of a mystic—Theresa of Àvila, the saint who lost her life because of where her visions led. She also made me think of an injured child or wounded animal. I could only imagine what it had been like to be kidnapped and then imprisoned in that drug house. That's when I realized: Parker probably had a weapon, too.

"Are you OK?"

She rubbed a hand over her mouth, her eyes resting on the gun. "Are you planning to shoot me?"

I stuck it away, helped her to her feet and started to leave.

"Wait," she said.

She swayed against me. So I stood there a second. It felt like we'd weathered a storm, as if we'd been tested, and now calm flowed our way, a special grace neither earned nor petitioned, but then I heard a motor grind to life and gears clunked.

Tires spun and I began running, my legs pumping through the

leaves. Crashing through the vegetation to the lip of the ditch, I saw him pull away. The Tasmanian devils looked as if they were bidding me good-bye.

"Good riddance," said Monica, appearing next to me.

"He was going to be our ride."

The truck bounced and jangled down the road, cresting a small rise and dipping out of sight. He obviously had another set of keys.

A half-hour later, I imagined Jesus racing with us down the two-lane as I headed for Grand Rapids. Hair flying, robes blowing in the wind, I pictured the Savior settled at my rear on the motorcycle. Jesus, close at hand, encouraging me on into the foggy night. But Christ wasn't nestled on the seat behind me. Monica sat there, arms wrapped around my belly, holding on firmly, but not too tight, no doubt still mad at me for stealing this Yamaha. I was mad at myself for, I now realized, leaving the gun on the ground back at the farm. Ultimately, it had been no use to me.

I'd knocked several times on the front door of the farmhouse, which was old and in bad shape with junk scattered all over the yard. When we got no answer, I had gone around back, where I saw a note taped to the jam of the screen door. Rusty, I'm at the Riverboat Bar. Stop by, it said.

Then I spotted the bike parked near the barn. It had a key in the ignition.

Monica wanted to try another farm, but none was in sight. Anyhow, I didn't want to, not tonight. I wanted to get going, and not be sitting ducks, alone on a country road. I told her we weren't too far from M-66, a main artery where we could find help and a phone.

As I rode, I kept my eyes out for that van, fearful Mohawk and Arnold were not going away and were more than likely apt to call in reinforcements.

Monica tugged on me now and I bent my ear in her direction.

"Slow down."

We were on a two-lane in farm country west of Lansing, about a half-hour drive from home. The odometer needle showed the bike pushing 80. An old hand at cycling, the speed didn't bother me. Instead it gave an outlet to all that had been building up. Flinging Parker's things at the van had been one thing, but careening along the highway on the bike was another. There was pure freedom and release in this—even if the circumstances were not in our favor.

But I geared it back to 65, noticing car headlights shoot our way from the west. They reached us in a flash, and then vanished. I wondered if it was Rusty and his buddy from the farmhouse returning from the bar.

Stars hung sharp as pinpricks in the sky, and fog had all but dissipated. Above us stretched a vast deep of black.

I recalled how I'd taken Monica a couple years ago on a cycle for a color tour of northern Michigan. It had been a wonderful weekend, filled with lots of cider and scenery and warmth between us. I knew she trusted me that time as I drove. It was different now. She was scared, and who blamed her.

As we rose from a tiny dip in the road, I spotted a clear straightaway and an orange glow in the distance – a gas station, civilization, and a phone.

CHAPTER TWENTY-TWO

We stopped at the intersection. I waited for the cars and trucks flying by on M-66 to clear before hanging a left and heading for the truck stop.

I pulled into a dark area in the back part of the lot, in which a handful of semis sat, diesel engines rumbling, exhaust curling from tailpipes into the chilly air. High-powered lights lit the gas pumps and grocery store by the road. I figured it to be going on 11 by now.

"It's cold," said Monica, swinging off the bike and blowing on her hands. The large collar of Dezi's buckskin coat obscured her face. Her teeth actually chattered. "Don't you feel it?"

If anything, I was hot.

Our feet crunched gravel as we wove between the semis and made for the pumps, but we hadn't gone far when Monica stopped, facing me, her body weaving. She put a hand to her chest.

I was alarmed and asked if she was OK.

She used my shoulder for support, bent her face to the side and got sick again.

I waited next to her.

Monica coughed.

I bent closer, thinking how she had been halfway around the world to preach, only to return home to this.

"OK," she finally said. "I'm ready."

Still, she stood and wavered, giving me a brave, lopsided smile. "This is another fine mess you've gotten me into."

Her humor offered me hope.

"We're just about in the clear," I told her.

But we'd only gone a couple steps when I spotted two truckers talking to a couple guys by the gas pumps. One of the men wore a long black coat. His hair had been shaved from the sides of his head. The other, even from this distance I could see, had muscles coming out of his ears. Beyond them a long white stretch limo idled, a back window down.

"Let's go," I said to Monica.

I pointed, noticing Mohawk and Arnold gazing toward the space between the trucks where we'd been only seconds before.

"Can you keep going?" I asked.

She nodded and wiped her mouth. "Do we have a choice?"

I took her elbow and trotted along the edge of the fence, staying in the deeper shadows, moving toward the cycle.

I raced out of the truck stop, shot down M-66 and then made a quick left at the two-lane that went west, toward Grand Rapids.

I checked the side mirror and spotted headlights, maybe a half-mile back. Already hitting 75 mph, I heard, "Calvin, watch out!"

Two raccoons waddled out of the weeds, dragging their striped tails with them. Four red eyes turned our way. I kept steady, made a slight adjustment, and we slipped right between them. I felt no thump, turning either of them, and possibly Monica and myself, into road kill.

Jockeying the bike close to the yellow line, I noticed a truck bearing down from the other lane. It roared by, its trailer shaking and rattling and buffeting us with wind.

But I kept a good grip on the bike, my mind racing. I'd driven this road, not on a motorcycle, several times. It paralleled the freeway that less than 48 hours before—it seemed like weeks—I'd taken to Detroit with Bob and Dezi. Fire bloomed for a moment in my mind and I recalled Bob and Dezi running from that explosion. Bob had put himself on the line to save his sister. I prayed he and Dezi were OK.

Approaching an intersection, I checked the mirror, saw lights back there again, quickly surveyed the road ahead and decided to blow the stop sign. Monica said something, but her words were lost as I whipped through without incident.

The mirror revealed no one.

Once again I ran through my head what I knew of this road. Its geography, until just outside of Grand Rapids remained rural: farms, fields, a church, a small lake, a cemetery.

Also, there was a youth home, which I'd visited to talk to teens in trouble, and next to that, maybe a mile down the road, a golf course.

I'd played 18 holes there once for a fundraiser for Hospice, and another time I'd attended a reception in a large banquet hall next to the pro shop. I'd married a young couple and they had asked me to give the prayer before dinner. Given my own unmarried state, officiating at weddings was always a trip. If I remembered right, there was a pay phone outside the pro shop.

I racked us up another few miles per hour, baffling out a storm of exhaust. Nothing showed in the mirror now.

Trees leapt by on both sides, a large army of them, and then things cleared on our right, revealing rolling grounds and the youth home in the distance. Soon we came up on the golf course.

I slowed, gearing us down, the cycle skidding slightly. Rags of fog now appeared, rising out of a swamp on our left. A final glance in the mirror showed darkness, and so I killed the lights, geared back as much I dared and swung off the road. Rolling into the parking lot, I made for pines lining one of the fairways. Nearly there, I dared a look over my shoulder and spotted lights beaming down the road.

We ducked into the pines and eased to a stop. Neither of us spoke, but we looked at the road, maybe 75 yards away.

A white car, its long snout of a hood leading the way, slid by the entrance we'd just taken.

"It's them," Monica said softly.

The taillights disappeared.

The night grew enormously still. The tang of pine and a lingering odor of skunk hung in the air. The cycle engine ticked as it cooled. Neither of us moved for maybe a minute.

"To think this time last week we were shopping in Amsterdam," said Monica.

"You and the Dalai Lama?"

She socked me in the ribs. "Ha-ha."

Pines towered over us. The golf course stretched in three directions. Maybe another 50 yards from us stood the clubhouse. A haze floated that way, but I made out the red and white glow of a Coke machine. "I think there's a phone over there by that building," I said.

I put my arm around her and we went that way.

"Calvin," Monica said, "do you really think Dezi is to blame for this?"

"A fair share of it."

"Back in Detroit, she insisted I take her coat. You don't think ..."

"I'm not putting anything past her, good or bad."

A few minutes later, Monica sat on a bench at the edge of the pond, near the 18th green. Sipping a Coke and eating a candy bar I'd gotten from the machines, she gazed at the water.

I took my Coke and candy to the pay phone while she rested. A handful of calls brought me to this one. Manny was nowhere to be found. I'd spun through a couple more numbers and then dialed Benny Plasterman, my friend the Barry County undersheriff, at home.

The phone was attached to a pole just outside the door to the pro shop. Golf bags and clothes were barely visible inside. I drank the rest of my pop and swallowed the remains of a Snickers bar. Luckily the machines took dollars, and I had a credit card to make these calls.

I finally heard, "Cal? What in the world is going on?"

"I need some help."

"Where are you?"

I scanned the dim fairways, the sky, the moon, the pond and Monica on the bench, maybe 25 feet in front of me. "Deer Run Golf Course," I answered.

"What are you doing there?"

"Running from a bunch of men from Detroit. I need your help, Ben, and the sooner the better."

Monica looked around at me. Then she turned back to the pond, on which moonlight fell, creating a small path shimmering from one side to the other. Maybe halfway out there floated a few swans.

"Who are these people from Detroit?" asked Ben.

I gave him the short version.

"They're after you right this minute?" he asked when I finished.

I told him they were, thinking it was a reflection of our friendship that he pretty much took what I told him at face value. He knew me, knew I wasn't lying, and knew I needed his help.

"Just a second," Ben said.

He put me on hold, which gave me a chance to dig in my pocket for a Baby Ruth, but my fingers slid across something small and hard. I pulled it out, recalling the wadded hankie and the ring I'd put in there earlier at the rectory.

Phone cradled to my neck, I picked it open and pulled out the ring.

Monica stood, facing me.

"I've got Ben Plasterman," I told her.

She nodded, sipping pop. A few years ago I had helped Ben track down a renegade cop who had helped kill a local history professor. Monica and I had been broken up at that time, but that's when we started to rebuild what we had lost.

Traffic hummed in the distance and I felt the cold air on my ears and hands.

"What's that?" Monica asked.

I handed her the ring. As she held it up in the light from a lamp behind the pro shop, I heard, "Calvin? I've called Kent County. They've got a man on the way. He's in Ada, so maybe it'll take 10 minutes."

Relief trickled all the way through me. Ada wasn't too far. "Thanks, Ben."

"Anything else?"

I asked him to call St. Anne's rectory in Detroit, to ask for a Father Zerba and to find out what happened to Bob and Dezi, and to track down Manny as well. I also decided to mention to him the call I had gotten from the WMU history teacher. After all, Ben had put me on to him.

"It sounds like he's looking for the reward, too," said Ben.

"Money talks."

170

Then, Ben said, "Cal. Since you bring it up, maybe I ought to tell you this for what it's worth. I talked to my guys and then went over their reports real closely on the murder of Melinda Blackwell."

I waited.

He went on. "There is some additional information from the guy at Western. It seems he saw Melinda in a bar south of Kalamazoo, not too long before her body turned up."

"You've known this all along?"

"Friend, do you want to hear this or not?"

"Sorry."

"She was in there with a guy who, from what I found from Manny Rodriguez, matches the description of the man who died in the cathedral. Also, there was another man there. A big guy, lots of muscles."

"Arnold?"

"Who?"

"Never mind. Go on."

"They were arguing in the bar, the two men, and then took it outside. Melinda went with them. The teacher at Western—I think he wasn't too forthcoming because of who he was at the bar with that night. He only came forward with this under duress. But, anyway, he stepped outside to see if she was OK. He saw them talking in the lot with another man, this one who apparently was driving a red car, maybe a BMW."

My mind raced and calculated. "Any idea who that was?"

"Not really."

"Go on."

"That's about it, Cal. I thought, maybe given what kind of soup you are in, you ought to know that much."

"Thanks."

"Look, you want me to stay on the line until the deputy shows up?"

"No, I'm OK."

Monica had walked back to the pond. She turned when I stopped beside her and handed me the ring. "Where did it come from?"

I told her.

"It's a Notre Dame Law School ring," she said.

"You read Latin?"

"It's not that hard."

I examined it more closely, holding it up and, in faint light falling our way from the pro shop, thought I glimpsed writing inside. I showed it to her.

"Initials maybe?"

I couldn't quite make them out, but I did get an idea.

Meanwhile, water lapped mud by our feet. The flag clinked on the pin in the hole on the 18th green. A rich smell of fertilizer rose to my nose. I put my arm around Monica, and she leaned my way. I thought briefly of New Orleans. What I'd done, or maybe failed to do.

"This ring could be important," I said.

"How so?"

"It's possible your brother found it the other night in a garbage bag."

"What?"

"I'll explain later."

We waited, watching those swans swim. Fears welled in me and so did a joy that came out of nowhere. "I'm wondering," I said, my thoughts veering in an entirely unexpected direction, "are we ever going to get married?"

Her eyes came to life. A smile opened, transforming her. "Is this a proposal?"

"Sort of."

She shook her head. "How about asking that later, when we're not so busy with, you know, other life and death matters?"

"But it's a possibility?"

"Could be."

"Even if I keep getting us into scrapes."

She put a hand on my head. "Calvin," she said, "God willing, I'll be able to change that part of you."

"And if not?"

"I'll pray for acceptance."

Suddenly, feathers flapped across the way, the swans stirring, as if detecting trouble. Then the surface erupted with spraying water, and a sharp, snapping sound cut through the air.

I grabbed Monica, pulled her down, covering her with my body.

Footsteps headed down the asphalt walk. When I looked up, I saw Mohawk. He stopped and poked his small automatic rifle close to my nose.

"Long time no see," I croaked.

He looked very serious.

More footsteps came our way.

"Ain't' that cute, two lovebirds," said another voice. It was Arnold.

As Mohawk stepped aside, I rose and helped Monica to her feet, but she swung away and stepped into Arnold's path. I suddenly realized he hadn't been talking to us. "Don't!" she yelled.

He shoved her aside and opened fire again, the bullets skidding across the water, tearing into the swans. I thought they had left.

Monica was on him, and so was I.

But Mohawk got between us.

"You killed them!" Monica yelled, turning to the pond, pointing at two small white lumps, necks outstretched, floating in the middle of the water.

"You, too, if you don't shut up," Arnold said.

"You violent psychopath!"

That did it. Arnold lunged for her, and I started for him, but Mohawk shoved him in the chest. Arnold stumbled, nearly losing his balance, and came to rest against a rack used in the summer for golf bags.

He swore. Then Mohawk swung around. "Let's go."

"Where to?" I asked.

"Just do it, or I let him do you like he did the birds."

Monica grabbed my hand and pressed hard. We walked around to the front. As we went, I heard Arnold grumbling, and a plaintive, almost painful cheeping coming from the pond. It sounded like babies.

173

CHAPTER TWENTY-THREE

Several years ago, I stood outside the funeral home in Alpena and watched Monica walk away. Bob had bopped next to her, animated, apparently not too upset that his mother had just died of acute alcoholism. Monica led him down a street, toward the Lake Huron shore. She wanted to be alone with him for a while.

I remembered that time, her retreating back, as Mohawk led Monica to the waiting Windstar, parked on the far side of the lot near the street. I let her go then voluntarily. This time I had no choice.

Arnold had me climb into a deeply padded leather seat of the limo. Across from me sat Jamal, expressionless. As soon as I got in, the car pulled out of the golf course parking lot, the van not far behind.

Jamal smoked a thin cigar, those dark eyes shielded now by sunglasses. "Who was shooting?" he asked Arnold, who had climbed in next to me.

"I had to scare them," Arnold answered. "They were going to run."

"He slaughtered two swans, among other things," I interjected.

Arnold raised a hand, as if to cuff me, but Jamal snapped, "Sit there and don't even breathe. Already you are a disgrace."

The muscle-bound clown's wide, fleshy face leaked sweat; his high forehead showed scratches, dried blood and bruises, probably from tonight's fire. He sank back in his seat, glowering at me, the automatic pistol in his lap.

A window behind Jamal shot down, revealing the front, where Alonzo, the black kid from Oscar's store, played chauffeur. This was like old home week. "Where to, Mr. Jamal?"

"Grand Rapids."

The kid's eyes slipped over me, and he nodded before the window became a barrier again.

Lights along the edge of both doors gave the space a little illumination. The tinted windows allowed for no outside view, making it hard for me to see if a sheriff's cruiser was nearby. Or that van.

Jamal took off the glasses and stuck them in the lapel pocket of his white suit coat. He wiped a hand over his glossy black hair. "No more smart talk, Reverend. We want the map."

"If you get it, then what?" I asked.

"You, your girlfriend, her brother and that big-mouth whore go free. I don't need you anymore."

"Bob's in that van?"

Jamal offered a slight nod.

"How is he?"

"Right this moment, everyone's alive."

The limo purred smoothly down the road. "Why do you think I know where to find the map?" I asked.

Jamal crossed a leg over a knee. He had doused the cigar in an ashtray. "My friend, I'm finished arguing with you." He jerked up a cuff and checked his watch.

Jamal then turned his attention back to me, taking a cellular phone out of the lapel pocket of his suit coat and beginning to tap out numbers. "Reverend, we will break one of your girlfriend's fingers every time you don't answer me." He said this very calmly, a death gleam in his eyes.

"If it helps, I want you to know I've called the police and they're already looking for this car."

Jamal said nothing for a moment, those eyes losing none of their danger. "If the police come, my friend, you'll never see your pretty blonde girlfriend or her stupid brother alive again."

I knew he meant it.

"Put Ricky on," Jamal said to someone on the other end of the cell phone.

I assumed he meant Mohawk.

"Ask Dezi where it is, or Wooly, or, hey, even Oscar," I said. "Or maybe Parker."

Jamal was deadpan, his mouth firm. "Who is Parker?"

"Doesn't he work for you?"

"You're talking crazy, my friend."

I had a hunch he didn't know Parker.

"Ricky, I want you to break one of the minister lady's fingers," Jamal said. He listened a moment before adding: "No, it doesn't matter which one."

"Wait," I said.

He put his hand over the phone.

I had to buy some time and so blurted out a thought that had come to me after talking minutes ago with Ben. "You do know that it is a good bet that our friend here killed Melinda Blackwell," I said, indicating Arnold with my thumb.

Arnold shifted and started for me, but Jamal snapped, "Sit!"

"I'll call you back," Jamal said and turned off his phone.

I suspected that I was reaching, but that Notre Dame ring and Ben's comments about the argument in the bar and the conversation in the bar parking lot put it together. It gave me an idea.

"Did you know that, Mr. Jamal?" I asked. "He probably killed Donny Johnson, too, or was in on it."

The man across from me grew very still, his eyes shifting from me to Arnold.

"He's lying."

By the shaky tone of Arnold's voice, I wondered if I guessed close to home.

"You killed that woman?" asked Jamal.

Arnold started to protest, but Jamal cut him off, reached in the inside pocket of his suit and pulled out a knife. He leaned across me and stuck the blade right under Arnold's chin.

Clearly, Arnold was scared of Jamal. Otherwise he would quite likely have picked up–or at least tried for—his gun to defend himself.

"Talk to me, you pig," Jamal ordered in an even, but deadly, voice.

Arnold's eyes peered down the blade. "The bitch was arguing with

176

me. She wouldn't give me the map. She buried it someplace by the river up there and wouldn't tell me where."

"So, you killed her," I said, turning his way, wondering if I could grab his gun and take care of both of these clowns.

"Mr. Jamal, it was an accident. She fell down and hit her head."

"And that killed her?" I asked.

Jamal said softly, "Back out of this, my friend."

The limo rolled along. I felt hot and already had made the next leap in the logic of what happened.

"You killed her?" Jamal asked, flicking the knife under his chin.

"I didn't kill the bitch."

Jamal sliced skin, causing blood to spurt.

Arnold grabbed for his chin.

"You idiot, why didn't you tell me?"

"Damn!" Arnold looked at his bloody hands.

"Why didn't you tell me?"

"We were only trying to help."

In the commotion, I could have gone for his weapon. Maybe it would have worked, but I had another plan. Thinking of that ring and those initials, and of a red car, I stuck out my hand. "Let me make a call."

Jamal looked at me.

"I may be able to find the map for you."

Less than an hour later, I cut across the street from a burned-out shell of a grocery store on whose charred, bricked sides showed a few Central American murals. In one of them, a plaintive Caesar Chavez stared out at me as the white limo drove off down Division Avenue, leaving me to my mission.

It was cold and I had to pull my jacket close. My body felt ragged and worn. Moving by the front of the Guiding Light Mission, I peered in the front door, hoping to spy a friendly face. But it was after midnight. All of the street people were tucked in for the night.

Jogging across Division and heading through the side lot of the

Catholic cathedral, I realized how alone I was. Idly, I glanced at the dark windows of the cathedral, thinking of the other night.

This was up to me and it was a very risky business. But it was my best and only shot. The phone call had led to a dead end, and my only option was not a very good one.

Basically, Jamal had agreed to blend into the background and let me have at it. He gave me 20 minutes and reminded me not to pull any funny business. I told him I was in no mood for joking. Before I hopped out of the limo, he warned me again that things would go quickly from bad to worse for his hostages if the police appeared. Arnold had still been busy tending to his wound.

I cut down Sheldon Street and crossed behind LaGrave Avenue Christian Reformed Church. A block up, at Cherry, I stopped in front of a red brick house, fronted by wrought-iron shutters around the windows, and double doors at the entryway.

I started for the front door.

I thumbed the yellow button by the door jamb, setting off chimes inside. The sound seemed to echo off into a deep empty space. When I had called here, three times actually, there had been only the same recording telling me to leave a message.

Maybe no one was home, I thought. But, parked in the driveway along the side, was Barry Lazio's red BMW. So I kept at it.

Finally, I heard a bark, followed by scampering feet, a low guttural growl and the sound of a dog's body slamming the door. The animal leapt again, fell and seemed to tumble and then commenced barking.

The street behind me was dark. Across the way, two blocks to the east, was the brightly lit tower of Saint Mary's Hospital's new cancer center.

"Damon, shut up!" I now heard inside. "Who's there?"

The dog kept right at it, beginning to hop against the door, rattling the handle and snuffling heavily. Then I could tell by the strangled gargling sound coming from the dog that Lazio had grabbed the animal by the collar.

"Barry!" I called through the thick doors. "It's Calvin Turkstra."

I pounded the door, detecting movement behind a tiny peak hole. "Open up!"

Damon yelped and throttled the door again. But then I heard paws skidding against the floor and the sound of something closing. Shuffling feet followed, coming my way on tile, and the door swung open a few inches. A light switched on over me. Another one showed on the man behind the door.

Barry was dressed in a white polo shirt and gray sweat pants. He blinked, scowled and stepped aside to let me enter.

The faint smell of spaghetti and olive oil swam toward me from further inside. The aroma crawled straight into my belly, filled only with candy, soda pop and anxiety. There was another smell, too, of booze, coming from the mayor.

Barry's round face was flushed, his thick black hair combed straight back, not a strand out of place. His eyes moved to the doorway behind me, and an expression of fear passed over his face. He swayed a little on his feet. "Who's with you?"

His voice was slurred.

"I'm alone."

He motioned me out of the way, reached around and shut the front door carefully, as if keeping evil spirits outside. Then he leaned against it.

Damon meanwhile began to beat himself silly against another door. "Pipe down!" Barry yelled.

A fierce non-stop barking came in reply.

"What do you want?"

The framed painting of Christ kneeling in the Garden of Gethsemane and sweating bullets of blood hung from the wall on his right. Near that was a depiction of the Holy Family—Joseph, Mary and Jesus. Catholics liked their pictures.

"Barry, we need to talk."

He flattened himself against the door again, as if pinned there by my words. He closed his eyes, and his head lolled a bit. "What do you want?" he asked, gazing at me with blurry eyes.

"I thought you and the chancellor might like an update on my progress."

He didn't react to my light-hearted, late-night banter. So I moved right along. "I'm looking for a map." I watched carefully to see how he took this.

A question and hint of surprise washed into his eyes, as if he wondered how I knew this, but then his expression went blank again.

"If I can't produce it, people are going to get killed."

An edge of alertness filtered into his face. "People have already died."

"I'm talking in the present tense, Barry."

He stood there, looking like a man in shock. Finally, he snapped out of it enough to say, "I don't know what you're talking about, Calvin."

"That's a lie, Barry, and you know it. Where is it?"

He closed his eyes, looking as if he was painfully reflecting on something. Then he shook his head, and placed his fingers against his neck.

I stepped close. "Where is it?"

He would have backed up even more, if he could have. His only defense was his 80-proof breath.

"Barry?" I asked softly. "For the love of God, help me."

But he shook his head, eyes closed. Damon whined, not making such a racket. Lazio looked as if he was going to get sick. "I wish I could help you."

My gaze flew for a moment to that picture of the sweating Christ, and then set on the Holy Family. Mary held a bundled Jesus in her arms. "Do you want even more death on your hands?"

He looked at me surprised.

"You left your law school ring in the garbage bag you dropped at Calvin College the other night."

He held up a hand, as if trying to see if he had lost the ring.

"It was you in the church, wasn't it, Barry?" I suspected he may have been the one who body-slammed me.

He stared at his empty ring finger.

"Did you kill that kid?" I asked.

My hands raised, and he saw them. They hung there, not a foot from his fleshy neck.

"Parker works for you, doesn't he?" I asked.

Barry shook his head.

Squeezing his soft flesh of his neck might get him to divulge more. But at what cost? How far was I willing to take this? And yet, lives were counting on me. Hands still raised, I leaned close, and asked, "Do you know where the map is?"

Lazio choked back what sounded like a sob. "I don't know, Calvin. I don't know."

"You were in the parking lot of the bar near Kalamazoo, just before Melinda Blackwell, was murdered, weren't you?"

He shoved me in the chest, but it wasn't hard. I stepped aside and he nearly stumbled. I suddenly noticed how quiet things were. Damon had stopped his racket.

"Barry, you are in lots of trouble. Don't make it worse."

He swung around and landed on his rear atop an end table next to a mirror. He stuck his face in his hands and began to cry. He was pathetic. I went over and grabbed him by the shoulders. I shoved him up and stared into his drunken face, engorged by self-pity. But I saw something else as well—a chink in his armor, a hint that he wanted to help. Then he said, "Parker was here, but he's gone."

"He does work for you?"

"I asked him to help."

"Help how?"

"Follow you and tell me what you found."

"Did he find the map?"

"Someone else did, in that woman's home. It was hidden real well."

"Is he working with someone else now?"

"No, he came here, wanting to get paid. I told him no deal without finishing what we hired him for."

"And what was that?"

181

Lazio's shoulders slumped, his upper body swayed, his head tilted to the side. His eyes lifted to some space behind me, possibly to that picture showing Christ's agony in the garden. "The other guy's …"

I waited.

"Look, Calvin, you need to keep me out of this? Can you do that? I didn't kill anybody."

I decided to lie and to try to get him on my side. I told him his involvement, if he didn't do any of the killings, didn't really matter. What did matter, right now, is for him to tell me what he knew about the map.

It took us 20 minutes, and two more stiff slugs, from a bottle in his kitchen, and then more threats from me before he told me, "The other guy's got the map. He went to the river. The kid who died in the cathedral— the Indian—had a fishing shack there. He made his girlfriend bury the thing there."

"What thing?"

"A deed of some kind, Calvin, for the Indians. For the land where they want to build their casino."

"Buried it, why?"

"He was some kind of Indian nut. He hated the idea of a casino. He apparently insisted on burying it in some kind of crazy ceremony. The girl didn't like that. I think that's why she got killed."

When I pressed, Barry told me that Parker had had a look at the map, and he knew where the fishing camp was located. "Is that where Parker went?" I asked.

"Yes."

CHAPTER TWENTY-FOUR

Once Barry clued me in on the river site, I went straight for his phone to call Manny. But Barry stopped me and, as we stood in his kitchen, started pleading again. He told me even more. I listened carefully to what he said, feeling mounting dread. When he finished, I knew I had to make a different call, and to play it as straight as possible.

I dialed Jamal's cell phone, hoping that I could now give him what he wanted. But he didn't answer.

As I hung up, I knew I couldn't wait. I told Barry I needed the keys to his car and, if he had one, a gun.

In exchange, I agreed to let him call Manny. As mayor of Grand Rapids, he had a lot to worry about and wanted to start telling the story from his perspective. I didn't care.

Given that Monica was still out there someplace, and possibly at the spot along the Grand River, that's where I headed in Barry's BMW. I should have called Manny myself, but I let that ride, thinking I didn't want to spook Jamal—wherever he was now—into doing something I would regret.

I knew where the fishing camp was.

Packing Barry's .357 Magnum, I raced down Fulton, crossed the Grand River and kept going. If I had passed a pay phone, I might have stopped to call Manny,

But pay phones, even in Grand Rapids, had gone the way of dinosaurs and the Model T. I reached John Ball Park, the city zoo, quickly and hung a left.

Two blocks down, I parked the car in a small lot leading into Kent Trails, a city jogging path, and started to trot along the asphalt path running next to a Coca-Cola bottling factory. Coming in the back way was the quickest approach.

I funneled my thoughts into one direction—Parker had gone here, and something told me that Jamal was nearby as well.

If he wasn't, I was in it deep. But this seemed my best chance to save Monica and Bob and, if she was in danger, Dezi as well. The only plan I had I was now following. I figured the reasons for why Barry had been involved would come out in good time.

Past the pop place, I dipped into a dark thatch of woods. The stacks, silos and buildings of a mostly abandoned gypsum mine appeared on the right. Gypsum was the powdery white rock that first brought people to Grand Rapids. Tunnels honeycombed this entire section of town.

Twisted, broken trees and the silvery movement of the river showed once I rounded yet another bend on the path. Years back, this had been a fairly primal place. Mound-building Indians, the Hopewell's, had lived here along the Grand back in the time of Jesus. Remains of their culture were buried in the soil on which we walked. I guess it made sense that Donny Johnson—Geronimo—would use it as a ceremonial ground in which to stash something.

Jogging along, I saw the river glint through the trees on my left. A couple hundred feet ahead, through a screen of trees, was the old railroad trestle—where I was headed. I couldn't see it yet. But I'd jogged through here many times when serving the church in town and knew its location.

Just this side of it, across the river, sat the fishing camp. Native Americans were known to gather there in salmon season.

I was in luck. Light flickered and leapt over there. That's where they had to be. Adrenaline pumped into my veins—not for the first time tonight. This was one of those times when I felt drawn forward beyond all reason. A situation that was shaping me, not me it, and God wanted me here.

I hefted the gun and checked the safety. I'd gone to the police firing range a few times with Manny, and had practiced with his big police-issue handgun and my Navy-issue .22 pistol. Only once or twice had I touched one of these Wild West weapons, and then never to fire them. Before leaving Barry's, I made sure to load it.

I hoped I wouldn't have to use the gun. Even so, I snapped off the safety.

The light grew larger and then I heard voices drifting my way across the water. I figured I would slip through the trees and get as close as possible to the railroad trestle on this side of the river. See who was there and what was what. I thought now that I should have insisted on calling Manny. Being so frantic, my reasoning was slipping. I wanted to save Monica and Bob. Forget everyone and everything else. But I wasn't sure if this was the best way. Maybe all I'd find over there were fishermen.

The ground grew soggy the closer I got. The skinny trees didn't provide much cover. But bushes and brambles helped to hide me. The trestle rose maybe thirty yards away, a coupling of bars and beams. The water moved swiftly underneath, the flames—from what I now saw was a campfire—reflecting here and there in rippling strands. I hoped Lazio was right, that in his sloppy drunkenness he wasn't lying to me about this spot.

I ducked under a branch, thinking again how this area was an ancient burial ground. The actual mounds were on the other side of the river, between Indian Mounds Drive and the freeway. Indians still had rights to fish for salmon along here. I thought of Donny Johnson, not wanting a casino, apparently, but causing deaths as a result. I wondered exactly what he would have told me if we had been able to meet at the cathedral.

Halfway to the trestle, and maybe ten feet from the river, I saw a vehicle over there, parked this side of the fire. But it wasn't a van, or a limo. It looked like a white pickup truck.

I saw a few figures, moving in and out of the shadows cast by the fire. I kept low, crossing wet ground, my feet sucking and pulling out. I tried to keep quiet, smelling the mushy stink of wet weeds and dead fish. I could now make out a shack—just a few boards slapped over a platform wedged into the fork of a large tree. The river ran three or four feet from me.

A handful of people shifted in and out of the slow-moving shadows from the fire. A light flicked on inside another vehicle, parked further back in the trees by the road. I saw white shiny side panels and a long sleek hood of the limo. Then, I watched as three men moved from it.

The ongoing rush of freeway traffic helped mask the sloshing sounds I made as I closed in on the bridge. Suddenly, the ground gave way and I nearly fell in a small sinkhole. Lucky to keep my balance, I stumbled into another stand of trees. Once, in seminary, we had taken a mixed group of suburban and inner city school kids to this area to talk about God, the environment and how the Indians had a theology that meshed very well with the many of the teachings of Christ. That day a white kid and black kid got lost. We found them near this camp, playing tag in the weeds.

The forms by the fire assumed a clear shape the closer I came. They weren't native fishermen, chugging down a few brews before returning for fish. One looked small and had a limp with stringy hair hanging from his head. Back to the river, he stood this side of the dancing flames.

Half concealed by bristling cattails, I went to my knees in the shallow water. Both hands clasped the weapon. My ears picked up a word or two, subdued but serious. Two, maybe three people made a half circle on the other side of the fire.

A soft thumping, feet walking on wood, moved my way from the trestle, looming less than thirty feet away. I thought I caught a glimpse of someone up there, behind one of the webbed iron girders, keeping guard.

My eyes strained to take in the scene across the way. To make out exactly who was doing what. The small guy waved his arms, weaving back and forth, almost wobbling into the fire. He was talking fast, explaining.

A person emerged from the other side of the fire, his body lit by the glow. He had a large build, a bandage on his face. It was Arnold. Voices rose, angry, intense, arguing. I heard Arnold yell, "Where is it?"

Then I heard a high-pitched yelp. It came from the small man, whose body suddenly swung into view. Arnold had him by the hair. Fire burned and flames flew in waves next to him. He yelped again. It was Wooly Bully. Arnold flung him to the ground.

"Let me go, you asshole!" he yelled.

Arnold kicked him. Then coming into view, a partially shaved head, that long black coat. Mohawk. Right next to him, Jamal. I could tell him by the cut of the white suit. I think Parker hung in the background.

More sound came from the bridge. I glanced up and over and saw a shifting. Who was that?

I heard more yelling. Arnold stepped up and grabbed a shank of Wooly Bully's hair, dragging him up. He screamed in pain and swore. It looked like Wooly Bully had somehow hit the jackpot, found out all he needed to know and had come here to uncover the document. But then his luck ran out.

Jamal said something, his voice calm, low, and lethal, addressing them both. But I couldn't make out the words.

"Shoot him," I then heard Jamal say, his words skimming across the water to me.

As Arnold took aim, I extended my arms. It was an ethical dilemma: I had little use for Bully. But killing is killing and we all have a soul.

Double-gripping the gun, I aimed high, and fired a deafening blast. The Magnum bucked me back, but I didn't fall. My feet were planted solidly in the mud. Arnold swung my way. I wasn't sure if he had shot Bully or not.

I pulled the trigger of the monster gun again, keeping my sights high, this time dropping them to the ground. Or, nearly everyone hit the dirt. If I wasn't mistaken, Wooly Bully slid over, and rolled into the river, like an otter.

Mohawk rose and tried to aim at him as he started to swim away. I pulled the trigger a third time. By now they definitely had my position. Before they could shoot at me, I dashed over and ducked under the bridge.

Immediately, I realized my mistake. Feet skittered above. Someone could start blasting through the wooden rails at me.

So I dove into a thick covering of trees, flopping on my belly in slop, keeping the Magnum raised. Time for me to get out of there. I'd done my good deed for the night. Time for me to call in the cops. And let them sort it out.

Bullets whipped, slicing through branches, slugging into wood nearby. I crawled away from the river, climbed to my feet and angled for deeper cover.

Jamal yelled as I plunged on and had to dodge a half-buried boulder. I took a quick breather, on my knees behind the rock. Trying to take in the scene behind me, I heard clomping on the bridge and noise in the woods as well.

Then more shots—sharp, quick and crackling—buzzed into bark and whizzed through the air not far from where I'd been a minute before.

Back on my feet, I edged on, trying to quietly move away from the commotion and to lose myself in the trees. Absurdly, I thought of Indians and whites skirmishing in places like this so many years ago. A war of wills, the strong ready to consume the weak. The whites had won the war and left the Native Americans to scrounge a living any way they could, in the case of those I knew it meant a crummy casino. All of this, I thought, turned on approval to gamble. The curse of the casino.

Then I thought of Monica, upset over the dead swan, ready to take on Arnold because of what he had done. Then I thought of those poor orphaned birds chirping, and of those lost kids in the weeds by this same river. I was the one who found them.

I stopped a moment and gazed through a clearing in the woods, across the shimmering river, to a line of traffic a couple hundred yards away. The Indian Mounds were out there, humps in the landscape, bones and weapons and other pieces of a lost culture buried within. I wondered what else had been buried here. Then I started to go.

"Stop!"

I froze. But the voice hadn't meant me.

As someone crashed through brush, I spotted quick, stumbling movement, and a flash of white, to my right.

I heard what sounded like a door opening and closing. Then an engine revved, backfired and came to life.

"They're getting away!" someone yelled.

Lights flashed, lancing through the woods. The vehicle, not forty feet from me now, had turned around, and as it did I saw the rectangular shape of a van.

Not too far ahead, it crashed through trees.

If it was Monica, I wondered if she was trying to her free and if it would be best to let her go.

But then in the sweep of the headlights I noticed a stoop-shouldered figure, Oscar, race from the trees, not to far from where I stood, and point a weapon. "Dolores, you damn whore, stop!"

I think Dezi drove, cutting quickly around a tree and smashing through the undergrowth between two pines, edging off and then back onto what looked like a two-track. The Windstar bore directly down on Oscar, who took careful aim. Maybe they didn't know he was there.

I needed to stop him and let that van go.

Nearly even with him on the road, I burst from the trees. Darned near falling, I shoved off with one foot, stretching and tumbling right into Oscar before he could fire on the van. The fat grocer spun, twisted and sprawled.

Meanwhile, the van blasted by, missing us by inches.

Oscar moaned, hardly moving. In the carpet of dark that the van left behind, I got to my knees, quickly enough to see the taillights racing away.

The Magnum had somehow melded itself to my hand. I realized now that as I'd sprung out at Oscar, I'd also snapped the barrel as I went, and I think it had smashed his nose.

He looked stunned, rolling over. Now he seemed to recognize me, and his hand moved, raising his gun. "Don't try it," I said, showing my larger weapon.

I got up, pointing down at him. "I'm not kidding."

He rolled the other way, as if to protect himself. Oscar whimpered and groaned, cursing the world.

Then I felt something sharp in the crook of my back. "You are dead meat."

My legs went rubbery. I should have known this noise would draw trouble.

"You hear what I just said?"

I shrugged.

"Drop the gun."

The thud of the Magnum falling sounded like a nail in my coffin. He shoved me away, grabbed, and picked it up. "I'll use this."

Arnold, a small revolver in one hand, the big gun now in the other, smiled.

I heard—and so did Arnold—a motor start back by the campfire. "Get up," he said to Oscar. "Tell them to wait."

Oscar rose more quickly than I would have predicted and, one hand holding his nose, started to trot off. He went fast, doubtless primed by fear.

"Tell them, I'll be right there," Arnold ordered, his face showing a quick, clear pleasure. A big chunk of gauze hung from his chin.

"Did you kill the kid in the cathedral, or was it the mayor?" I asked.

He didn't answer.

"What's the matter, Mr. Universe, cat got your tongue?"

He raised the small gun, poised it in the middle of my forehead.

My world grew dark. I felt blood course through me, thought of Christ on his cross as the purple clouds gathered. Thought of myself on a cross years before, strung up by so-called friends, in the woods at grade school Bible camp. A prank that still haunted me. But I got out of that one. Weak-kneed, I stayed on my feet.

"What is your name really?" I asked Arnold.

"You are a dead man," he said and his finger pulsed on the trigger.

We stood there, suspended in a horrible interlude.

But then Arnold's eyes popped wide, the whites turning into eggs. He gagged and started to go limp. Two thick arms had straddled his neck and above one shoulder I saw a bruised and bloodied face, the eyes nearly swollen shut.

Arnold's arms flopped and his legs dangled. I watched his body go lifeless, the head drop, and the tongue start to loll. Behind him I heard a roar, anger pouring out.

Arnold's eyes turned to me, his body a couple feet off the ground, Bob's arms strangling the life out of him. I wished him all the luck in the world trying to break free from Bob's vice grip. But then I heard voices in the woods and sound of twigs cracking. Revenge is mine, the Lord says, and so I figured we better leave that to him.

"Monica and Dezi are free," I told Bob. "Let's go."

"No!"

"Do it, Bob."

Bumping Arnold from behind, Bob lifted and then let him drop. Monica's brother's clothes were tattered, shreds of tape hung from his wrists.

More noises and figures approaching made me make a quick business of it. I grabbed Bob's arm and yanked him hard. He wobbled, staring down at Arnold, on his back holding his neck, gagging.

"Let's hit it"

191

CHAPTER TWENTY-FIVE

The land rose steadily away from the river. Butterworth Avenue, I knew, looped along the far edge of this desolate area, running in front of the gypsum mine. Gravel and sand pits, oil fields and a few homes stretched that way as well. So that's where we headed, clomping through leaves and slogging through and around thatches of brush and bramble.

My clothes were muddy and wet; my chin throbbed, and a pain in my ankle came to life. But we were free, and it sure looked like Monica was, too.

Up ahead, through a gap in the trees and beyond a tall fence, I spotted the tail end of the mining operation. We slipped through and on to the road. Bob stopped and glanced around, wondering which way to head. His face, cut in several places, looked like it had been blotched with pepper.

Rain started to fall, and I hunched my shoulders as we crossed Butterworth and started along the shoulder of the road. Sandpits rose on the left. The gypsum mine—the only one still open in this area—spat steam and ground its gears. I felt cold, tired, my body beaten. I thought for a second of sacred springs that had once been located near here, soothing, medicinal waters that poured from the side of a hill and in years past drew the Indians for ceremonies. I ached to think of a people relegated to slot machines and blackjack tables for their salvation.

Bob plodded ahead, his big body slumped. He looked pretty bedraggled. I needed to get him to the hospital to have his head checked.

"Get out of the way," I said when a car approached, shooting from under the viaduct ahead.

The tires whooshed toward us on the pavement. A bolt of fear shot through me. What if turned put to be Jamal and his boys?

It wasn't. But I did recognize the vehicle that pulled to a stop and the window of the Tracker slid down. "Reverend?"

Frank Zerba sat behind the wheel, checking us over. "How's your partner there? We got separated in Detroit during the fire."

In answer, Bob puffed out his chest and put a hand over his heart.

A sweep of headlights came from behind. I gave them a look. We were still safe. But who knew what the next vehicle held, or others behind it.

"Climb aboard."

Zerba started off once we got in. Dashboard lights colored the priest's face with a wan, green glow. I checked on Bob in the back. He had closed his eyes, getting some rest.

Zerba drove the winding, dipping road. Rain beat on the windshield and the wipers slapped it away.

"So what brings you to Grand Rapids, Father?" I asked. "Not that I don't appreciate the ride."

He shot me a quick glance, then peered in the rear-view mirror. "We've someone to meet."

"Who is that?"

We drove by the entrance to Millennium Park, a large, riverfront park that Barry Lazio and his buddies in county government had been building.

"Father?" I asked.

He held up a hand as his cell phone rang. He grabbed it from his console and said, "Hello?"

I heard a muffled voice on the other end.

"Right," Zerba said. "I just went past the park."

Rivulets of water wiggled down the windshield, reminding me of tears.

"Where?" Zerba asked.

More muffled words.

"OK."

The priest slowed and started down a road between an empty field and a large area with a few small oil pumps. Flames from valves venting the ground licked the air.

"Father, who was on the phone?"

"We're almost there," he said.

Zerba slowed and turned down a two-track that wound toward the pumps. A gravel pit, its surface alive with spatters of rain, opened on the left.

We stopped next to a tall oil storage tank. The priest killed the lights, then flashed them twice, before turning them off for good.

Zerba rolled down his window. "Hello," he called.

"Who is it?"

"The priest from Detroit you were just talking to."

Peering out, I noticed movement on the metal ladder leading to the top of the tank. The figure paused and started down. He approached warily and stopped near the priest's window. He looked very fidgety, his drenched clothing hanging loose on his scarecrow frame. I'd seen him awhile before, by the fire, and then watched as he had slid into the water. "What're they doing here, Father?" he asked, meaning Bob and me.

"They're with me," Zerba said.

"Crap," said Wooly Bully.

"If it matters, I'm the one who saved your life back by the camp-fire," I said.

Bully dragged a hand through his stringy hair. "That was you?"

I nodded.

"I'll be," said Bully.

"So, Wooly, I heard you broke into an apartment in Detroit," I said.

He peered in at me. "We'll need to talk about that reward?"

"How so?"

"Well," he said, dragging what looked like a wet leather sack out of his back pocket. "It looks like I've got what everybody wants."

"Bully, you're going to be lucky if you stay out of jail," I said.

He stepped back, into the darkness. "You want this or not?"

Zerba's took out his wallet and began removing bills. "Father," I said, "who are you working for?"

Zerba looked at me, but didn't answer. He counted the cash, then reached out to fork it over. "It's all there," said the priest.

Bully stepped closer and snatched the money. "Three thousand?"

"As agreed."

Then Bully shoved the small sack through the window, and gave it to Zerba.

Bully bent and looked in at me. "Where's Dezi?"

"I have no idea."

"We'll be talking," he said and trotted off into rain that had suddenly started to fall in sheets. The smell of oil slipped in the Tracker and mingled with the other odors.

We sat there a moment. "Who're you working for, Father?" I asked.

"It's a long story."

"Is it the mayor, Barry Lazio?"

"It's someone in your bishop's office."

"The chancellor?"

Without speaking, Zerba switched the car around and drove back down the two-track. The Tracker bounced in ruts. Plumes of gas waved in the air. Rain slashed against the windshield. Questions tumbled through my brain. More than anything, I wanted to see the contents of the bag, which the priest had rested between us on the console.

"Frank," I said. "Can I look in there?"

He held up a hand and braked suddenly.

We had just reached the end of the two-lane, ready to turn on the main drag, when someone in a hooded rain slicker emerged from a clump of trees. The man's big torpedo of a body blocked our path. Through the driving rain, I saw him reach into a side pocket and swing an object our way. I was just about to warn Bob to hit the floor, and to do the same myself, when a bright light burst through the window on us. It was a high-beam flashlight, catching us in its glare.

Bob had awakened and started rocking my seat.

"I think it's the police," the priest said.

Rain fell on the roof, drumming a deadly beat. I used my hand as a visor, trying to make out who it was.

He sloshed through the watery two-lane to Zerba's side. The priest rolled down his window, and then the intruder yanked off his hood and stuck his face close to the window. Water dripped from his skin. His skull was shiny. "Turkstra, I should have known!" he thundered.

I sank in my seat. Had Police Chief Ray Kroger been out there all along, witnessing the transaction, or did he just come upon us?

"C'mon, you get out," Kroger said, yanking open Zerba's door.

The priest gave me a weak smile, grabbed the pouch and went out into the rain with the police chief.

Frank Zerba retraced our path, sliding between the oil pumps and empty farm fields, and then turning up Butterworth, headed toward the dump and downtown.

I hoped and prayed Monica and Dezi were safe. Before he raced away, I asked what Kroger wanted. Outside, they only talked for a minute or so, Kroger's voice a loud rumble, and then he left, taking the sack with him. His presence was strange, but everything was strange. It was like I was riding a car around curves that kept switching back and then switching again. It looked as if everyone was to blame.

"You shouldn't have given it up without a fight, Father," I said.

Rain slapped the windshield as Zerba took a wide sweeping curve, running between rows of tall pines.

"What was he doing out here alone anyway?" I wondered.

"The chancellor sent him."

"You're kidding?"

The priest rubbed his face with a free hand. Bob was already back asleep.

"Father, who are you working for? The cardinal? The chancellor? Jamal?"

He stayed quiet, driving along. "Right now, Reverend, a simple thanks for giving you a ride in this rotten weather will suffice."

I wanted more. The road ahead looked slick and shiny; the sky blurry. I asked, "Frank, do you have any idea what was in that pouch?"

"Actually, no."

"Don't you care?"

Zerba wouldn't say.

I watched the rain wiggle its way down the windshield, hearing Bob snore. "And does the police chief work for Jamal?"

Zerba didn't answer for second. "It's very complicated, Reverend. You wouldn't believe—from what I gather—the number of people who don't want that casino built."

"Why?"

He glanced at me. "Competition."

"And the Catholic Church cares about that?"

"I thought you hated gambling?" he asked.

"If so?"

"Then why worry about what it takes to keep another one from opening?"

"Because, Frank, the Indians in Wayland have been screwed for all of their lives. They don't need to go through it again."

"Even if it means putting all of their hopes in a gambling casino?"

"Yeah, even if."

"What changed your mind?"

I shook my head.

"Truth is, Reverend, I'm not sure who will win out with what's in that sack. If you ask me, too many people have been hurt whatever the hell it contains."

I felt sick to my stomach, hating the thought of what one group would do to keep another from getting its due. But then the whole business was dirty.

"Frank," I said.

But he braked, nodding out the windshield.

Walking on the side of the road was a man in a dark coat. I recognized the cocky stride. He turned our way, shielding his eyes, as we approached.

"Stop," I said.

Zerba slowed, shooting past Manny Rodriguez, then he pulled over on the side of the road. The cop trudged our way in the side mirror. I popped my door and hopped out.

I feared, as needles of rain scraped my face, that much of what had happened, the real motivation for the two deaths, was going to evaporate, much like tonight's fog, leaving in its place official lies and explanations. I felt a slow turning inside of me, the sense that somehow I helped to move along all of this mayhem—and to no good end.

I waited for Manny by the side of the Tracker. We watched each other carefully as the space between us shortened.

A couple cars slid by, their tires spewing up water. This part of Butterworth, maybe a mile from the dump, was thickly wooded, making things seem much more remote than they were.

"Well, well, if it isn't my favorite Protestant busybody."

Rain dripped from his face, his baseball cap looked sodden. His mustache bristled wetly. Hands stuffed in the front pockets of his jeans, he pulled up short of me. At that moment, Zerba gunned the engine. Smoke swirled out of the tail pipe. "Who've we got in there?" asked Manny.

"A priest from Detroit, and Bob"

Manny nodded, taking off his cap and smacking it on his thigh, which made drops of water fly. He then stuck it back on, backwards, adjusting it as if it really mattered.

"I don't suppose you're out for a late night walk in the rain?" I said.

Drops fell between us, pooling in puddles on the shoulder of the road.

"Actually,'" he said, gazing beyond me. "I've been busy saving your hide." He looked at me, mildly interested in my reaction.

"How so?"

"Perhaps you heard some of the shooting back there?"

"That was you?"

He held out his hands. "The one and only."

"Did you hit anything?"

Manny wiped a finger over his mustache. "I might have winged a white limo."

"What brought you out here?" I asked.

"Believe it or not, Reverend, police work," he said.

It was chilly; the dark seemed to wrap around me like a very cold blanket. Something that felt like fever tickled my throat. Zerba sat quietly in the truck, so did Bob.

"We just had a brief but very productive meeting with your boss," I said.

The rain eased for a moment. Steam from our breaths hovered above us, mingling with the exhaust from the Tracker. Manny blew on his hands.

"He took the bag that the priest in there came across."

Manny seemed to chew on this a second. "Bag?"

"The object of all of this mess."

"What's in it?"

"Ask Kroger."

The rain had shifted into a fine haze. Sirens screamed in the distance.

Manny gazed at me like he wanted to say more on the topic. But he didn't. Instead, nodding at the Tracker, he asked: "You and your friend, the priest, going to offer me a ride?"

CHAPTER TWENTY-SIX

The doctor worked meticulously to remove slivers of glass from Bob's forehead. I sat in a chair and tried to offer Monica's brother support.

But he didn't really seem to need it. His hands folded on the hospital gown over his belly, Bob could've been undergoing an extensive shave and haircut. His eyes locked on the ceiling, the trickles of blood barely visible now along the sides of his face. I think the drugs helped. When we got here he'd been woozy, but he had perked up. He wasn't, however, out of the woods.

The doctor pulled a half-inch needle of glass from Bob's cheek. "Any more like this and we're going to the OR."

A nurse bustled in to check the metal container in which the doctor had been sticking glass. All the shards came from the exploding house in Detroit. On the way here in the Tracker, as Manny and Zerba talked, he had dug open two big cuts.

"This man's lucky none got in his eyes," said the physician, whose name was Nancy.

Bob's head rolled her way. He smiled. "Snappy."

The doc gave me a curious glance. I shrugged.

She returned to work.

Manny had dropped me off an hour or so ago, promising to be back soon to talk. He took Father Zerba with him to the cop shop, probably to find Kroger. The Grand Rapids police captain also said he would try to track Monica down and tell her where I was. Hearing a familiar voice in the hallway, I stood and stretched.

A nurse came in, looking concerned, and said there was a friend out there, asking how things in here were going.

200

"That's not a friend, that's a news reporter," I replied as Randy VanderMolen, The Press religion editor, stepped into the room.

The nurse started to read him the riot act.

"It's OK," I said wearily to the nurse.

The Press guy stood next to me, rocking on the heels of his squeaky shoes. His hair looked like it had just finished a run through a wind tunnel and he wore a silly tie showing Tweety Bird. "So, Turkstra, how's the world been treating you?"

Dr. Nancy kept picking away. "It's getting crowded in here," she said without turning.

VanderMolen, looking a little embarrassed, turned to me for advice.

We went out.

The hall looked busy on this early Friday morning. Doctors checked charts; technicians wheeled machinery up and down the hall, and a couple of paramedics rushed in pushing a stretcher on which an elderly man moaned.

VanderMolen leaned against a wall. "How's your friend?" He nodded at the room in which Dr. Nancy's back and Bob's twiddling toes were visible.

"He's pretty banged up. The doctors may want to keep him. They're worried he might have gotten a concussion."

The reporter's eyes grew large and he nearly licked his chops. "That's from the explosion at the crack house in Detroit, am I right?"

"Randy, what are you doing here?"

VanderMolen nonchalantly pulled his notebook out of a back pocket. "I came in early, and they sent me over here, seeing that you and I go back a ways. We can still get something in for today if we hurry."

I took a spot next to him on the wall, my head thumping with pain, my eyes bleary. "I'm sorry, but I don't have anything for you."

He had snapped open his ballpoint and scratched two words—explosion, Detroit. "C'mon, Reverend," he said. "I heard there was a gun battle on Indian Mounds Road last night and that you were in the thick of it."

I closed my eyes, seeing me on that motorcycle and Monica by that pond, gazing at the swans. "I don't know anything about that," I answered.

"That's not what I'm told. Reverend, you know me. I won't burn you." VanderMolen blinked, pen poised over the paper. Tweety Bird was paying attention as well.

When a reporter says he won't burn you, it's time to put on your asbestos suit. "Ask Captain Rodriguez."

The religion guy drew a question mark on his pad. The nurse strode by and glared at us. We were definitely breaking the rules, conducting an interview in the ER.

"Does any of this have to do with that white limousine the cops were chasing this morning? The one with Detroit mob guys in it," VanderMolen asked.

This was news to me, and I wanted to know more. "Mob?"

"Maybe not exactly Mafia, but close."

I had to admit that I wasn't surprised. "Did they catch it?"

"I haven't heard." The reporter tapped the pad with his pen. He gave me an I'll-scratch-your-back while you-scratch-my-back look. "Reverend, this is a very big story."

I stepped from the wall, noticing Dr. Nancy wiping Bob's busted brow with a towel. "Tell me what you've heard?" I asked.

"What about this old letter or something we're hearing about?" asked the reporter.

"Letter?"

VanderMolen scratched behind an ear with his pen. "Our business editor is clued in tight with the anti-casino guys and he heard something about a document or something written by an old Indian chief."

"What's it about?"

"I hear it dates back to the late 1800s and maybe says something about land and even gambling."

"If that's what it is, will it matter?"

"Heck, yes. The current court case is about that, the location."

"If the location is right, then the Indians in Wayland are home free?"

VanderMolen shrugged. I was about to ask him another question when I heard voices rumble down the hall, by the nurse's desk, one booming louder than the others.

Spying me, Chief Kroger started down the hall, looking like a pit bull, gathering speed as he came. The police chief stopped short of me, his breath stale, and cheeks grizzled and ruddy. "Are you talking to The Press, Pastor?"

"As far as I know, Chief, it's still a free country."

Kroger's uniform looked wrinkled and stained. Mud caked his boots. He smelled like oil.

"Get out of here. Get, scram," the police chief said to VanderMolen. "We'll talk to you later."

The reporter refused. "What do you know about a historical document, Chief, maybe something that the girl they found in Gun Lake a while back had uncovered."

All of this had been over an old letter.

"How about it, Chief? Is all of this about the casino in Wayland?"

Kroger nearly went berserk. "If you print that, your paper is in deep trouble."

"Is it true?" asked the reporter.

The police chief turned to me, looking furious. "What did you tell him?"

"The truth," I answered, which was a lie.

Doctors and others had stopped and were looking at us. "You don't tell him anything. Right now, you have a lot of explaining to do."

His face bulged with anger. All of his rage narrowed, swelling his chest and coiling in his arms. "We're going back to the station. You and me, we're going to talk."

"And you're going to tell me why you came out of nowhere to snatch the sack?"

This about sent him into the stratosphere.

"Reverend!" He leaned closer, swinging a dismissive hand in VanderMolen's direction.

I wanted to lash out, to defend myself, to put him in his place. But suddenly he grew foggy. I slumped against the wall. I'd been plenty banged up the last few days—maybe I ought to get checked for collateral damage. I had to wait a few seconds for the feeling to pass.

"Turkstra,'" Kroger said in a low growl, ignoring my medical condition. "Do you think it's over?" His breath smelled now of peppermint. His face was so close I saw the pores around his flat nose. "It's not, not by a long shot."

I wanted to keep grilling him on why he was out there alone in the rain to get the sack. But I wasn't up for it. "Chief, I've had it, with everything, you included."

"Then what are you doing holding a press conference?"

I felt light-headed again. "Anything else?"

I closed my eyes.

"You took the letter out of that sack, didn't you?" he said in a horse whisper.

I opened my eyes and saw more than anger—confusion, accusation.

Then I heard more voices down the hall. Images from that fire, that awful ride in the bed of that truck, Wooly's body around that fire battered me.

"Turkstra? Am I getting through?"

Everything felt fuzzy again. Kroger's voice echoed, bounced around, didn't really settle. His face stretched so close to mine that I thought he was a funhouse mirror. Inches from me, he kept looking, as if trying to read something burned on the hardpan of my skull. "Where is it?" he demanded.

I shook my head, trying to make it all make sense.

He grabbed my arm and yanked. "Let's go. Back to the office."

My head buzzed. My legs wobbled. Poor Bob, racing for that house, and being blasted by glass. Now the doctor was tweezing ugly pieces from his face. Then there was Dezi, on that mattress.

I heard my name.

Monica ran down the hall, slipping through doctors and nurses. I went around Kroger for her, noticing the smudges on her face, the tattered sweater, that short hair. She stopped as I reached out my arms.

Then Kroger wedged between us, acting as a roadblock. "Wait right there, Reverend," he ordered.

But Monica dodged his upraised arm, looking anxious and scared and happy at the same time. We embraced. When she broke away, she asked, "That was you, wasn't it, back by the river?" she asked.

I nodded.

"Where's Bob?"

"In there, getting fixed up." I pointed.

She looked that way. "Is he going to be all right?"

"I think so."

"Are you?"

"I'm fine."

Monica nodded, checking me out, then started for her brother. But Kroger held her. "Not so fast."

I lunged, ripping on his arm, tearing it from Monica and spinning him around. The big cop nearly stumbled, but then he reached for me. I, however, was wilting, like a tree in hot, hot sun.

Thankfully someone intervened. "Chief," said a voice, "calm down."

I tried to move, but stumbled. "You too, Turkstra."

"No argument from me."

Kroger breathed hard, his skin bright red, sweat on his brow. Manny Rodriguez stood between us. He led his boss away.

Now Dezi appeared, her cheeks showing bruises.

I closed my eyes, feeling my head turning into a tilt-a-whirl. But then they opened, and I saw Monica intently speaking to Dr. Nancy. Bob sat up on his stretcher, gazing out at us—well, at Dezi to be exact.

Dezi leaned close. "Did you kill Oscar?"

"No, but he might have a broken nose."

This lifted her mood.

VanderMolen shoved close, brandishing his pad, not failing to take in the upper realm of Dezi's tattoos. "Miss," he said, "can I ask you a question?"

She glanced at his pad, snitched it from his hand and flipped it at the wall. "No way, Jose." Then she pivoted, shoved by and into the room to check on Bob.

Down the hall Manny and Kroger were arguing, very loud. I heard the police chief say, "Not a thing. That thing was empty."

VanderMolen had retrieved his pad and, edging toward the cops, wrote madly. I wished him well and then sank to the floor. Not really out of it, but no longer really with it either.

CHAPTER TWENTY-SEVEN

Monica slept, her breathing soft and even. The clock next to her bed read a little after midnight. Her odor, a powerful but sweet mixture of soap and bath powder, filled the room.

It had been a long day, much of it spent first in the hospital and then at the police station, where I answered questions. Today's newspaper had carried a hastily written story, touching on some of last night's events and mentioning that the source of all the action—a mysterious historical document—had been the cause of turmoil, and yet remained missing.

Dezi had been with us in the hospital, but then disappeared. We had brought Bob back early this evening, after they released him. We had eaten dinner, spent time talking and doing a little praying, and then Monica drifted in here. When I came to check on her, after helping Bob get settled, I saw she had fallen asleep atop the covers.

I found a quilt, laid it over her and, intending to just rest a moment before writing a note and heading home, sat in this chair by the window and conked out. I had now been up for awhile, staring at the ceiling and ruminating.

My thoughts had ranged far and wide. In many ways, things kept coming back to the letter. I had gotten it from Frank Zerba, who showed up at the hospital this afternoon, long enough to give it to me and explain how he had been able to slip it out before giving the sack to Kroger. My bet was that the folks who wanted to block the casino saw this for what it was—a solid tool to help convince the public and others that the land in question could, by the will of one of the tribe's fathers, be used for gambling. Money from the enterprise, it was hard for anyone to argue, could go a long way toward preserving the native culture and providing important services to the tribal members.

I carefully pulled the letter from my shirt pocket and read it over again. Written in strong, dark script, it described the location of the ancestral land for the Gun Lake Tribe of Indians and then went on, in the words of the tribe's chief, to offer hope and advice for the future. The letter I had looked to be the original. Crafted on thick paper, it had held up well. The leather sack had kept it dry.

"Cal?" I heard from the bed. "Did you put the quilt on me?"

"Yes, ma'am."

Monica stirred, sliding up in bed and resting against the head-board. This setting, so intimate, here in her room, felt uncomfortable and reminded me of the distance still between us. We sat in silence awhile. I could feel her looking at me. Once again, I recalled her at the pond, watching the swans. As far as I knew, Jamal and his boys left town without much of a trace. But I didn't suspect they would get away. Then again, maybe they would.

"Do you feel like talking?" Monica finally asked.

I scooted up in the chair, glanced out at a sea of carports in the lot of her apartment complex. The light spread like a vague blanket on the roofs of cars and storage areas. Further back stood a clump of trees and a small nature path that Bob like to prowl, pretending to be a big game hunter. In his room now, he had bandages and stitches all over his face.

"I can't believe what's happened," she said.

"It's going to take awhile to sort out."

Monica wore an outsized Hope College sweatshirt, and had her hair pulled back with a rubberband.

"Are you reading the letter again?" Monica asked.

It sat in my lap. I nodded.

"You really think it's authentic?"

"I'm betting."

Manny had told me he was planning to bring the mayor in for questioning, but that Barry was for the time being unavailable. I had no idea what that meant. I planned to tell Manny about the letter, after I gave it to one of the men in my church who was the brother of the tribal chairman. It seemed strange—I had been a vocal opponent of the casino, preaching against it more than once, and now I was quite likely going to play a role in getting it up and running. God, most assuredly, worked in weird and wondrous ways.

Monica shifted on the bed, making room for me. "Please?" she asked.

I got up and sat on the edge of the bed, reached over and took her hand. I had to admit, she was a trooper. "So, where to from here?" she asked.

"I've called Bill Blackwood, the tribal chief's brother, and told him I'd drop it off in the morning."

"You really think it will make a difference?"

I had brought the letter to her bed with me, and so handed it to her.

"If they can make sure it's not a forgery or fake, it might," I said.

She read it over, nodded and pointed. "Does this surprise you?"

She meant the final paragraph that said that the tribal land, although once used for hunting, may turn to other purposes in the future. Whatever uses, said the letter, they ought to always be done with the future of the tribal people in mind. The important thing was the people and their survival. It said nothing about gambling, but it was easy to read it as a charge, written by an important leader, to use that land to better the lives on those who owned it.

"How do you think this could help?" Monica asked, carefully folding and handing it back.

"It states the case in a way that's hard to ignore."

"It will matter?"

"Every little bit helps."

"Who do you think buried it by the river in the first place?" asked Monica. "I mean, was it always there?"

"Frank Zerba thinks Melinda buried it there to keep it away from folks in Detroit."

"So, she wrote the map to it?"

209

"It looks like," I said, aware of how many questions were yet to be answered. "Frank says she mailed it to Mary Simon, for safekeeping. I guess she knew Mary and liked her."

"Where did Melinda come up with it to begin with?"

"Not sure."

"How about the guy who died in the cathedral. Do you think he had a map to give you?"

"I don't think so; otherwise, Arnold and the rest would have had it and we wouldn't have had all of this grief."

Monica leaned close and I looped an arm around her.

A large dresser with an oval mirror stood against the wall on the other side of the bed. My reflection was in there somewhere, lost in shadows, trying to work its way out. I felt her hand press mine.

The apartment was silent around us.

I couldn't help thinking about that weekend in New York. It seemed so long ago, and yet so powerfully real. The feelings it created still pulsed between us.

Monica turned to me in the dark. I could feel the weight of her seriousness. I wondered if she had been reading my thoughts, and apparently she had. "I'm not sure I want to go on like this." She paused, staring hard at me.

"I thought you wanted me to sit here," I said.

"Don't joke."

She fell silent, maybe thinking of that night in New York. We had wine and did some dancing, strolled through the Village and ended back in her room. We had kissed, both surprised by the intensity of the feelings that we shared. I'm not sure exactly which of us backed off first, but we did.

We definitely were on our way to the bed. We both knew it and felt it. The joy and awesome responsibility that comes with sexuality was right there in front of us.

Things were never as black or white as we'd like to make. And yet, especially in the faith that we shared in Christ, there wasn't as much gray area as we'd like to imagine either. Bottom line, we'd been playing with fire, and knew it.

I left that night for my own room, feeling empty and hollow, aware that in the passion of our kissing, powerful needs were kindled. I could barely imagine the remorse we'd both have experienced if we had made it to the bed. It was obvious then, and obvious now that we were way beyond a crossroads. We were a couple in crisis.

I knew now we had to take this to God. We should have done it long before this. Not to have done that was madness.

Although we'd been together on and off for years, we had remained celibate—an amazing accomplishment in our sex-obsessed society. But the sex part was there, rearing its head, reminding us we were human, that we had needs, and that we had better start facing who we were and what we wanted together.

From her side of the bed, Monica cleared her throat. "When you asked about us getting married, did you mean it?"

We live in a day and age of uncertainly. Even some of us who have the certainty of salvation are unsure. I knew I'd better get off the fence and stand on the solid ground my faith assured.

I thought of us by that pond and of the swans that had been killed. I thought of how happy I'd been to see her in the emergency room. I thought that falling off the fence may not be such a bad thing, after all. "Yes, ma'am, I definitely did."

Now as for the Dalai Lama …